D1017497

SUNSET
IN
ST TROPEZ

www.**booksattransworld**.co.uk

Also by Danielle Steel

THE COTTAGE	HEARTBEAT
THE KISS	MESSAGE FROM NAM
LEAP OF FAITH	DADDY
LONE EAGLE	STAR
JOURNEY	ZOYA
THE HOUSE ON HOPE STREET	KALEIDOSCOPE
	FINE THINGS
THE WEDDING	WANDERLUST
IRRESISTIBLE FORCES	SECRETS
GRANNY DAN	FAMILY ALBUM
BITTERSWEET	FULL CIRCLE
MIRROR IMAGE	CHANGES
HIS BRIGHT LIGHT: *THE STORY OF NICK TRAINA*	THURSTON HOUSE
THE KLONE AND I	CROSSINGS
THE LONG ROAD HOME	ONCE IN A LIFETIME
THE GHOST	A PERFECT STRANGER
SPECIAL DELIVERY	REMEMBRANCE
THE RANCH	PALOMINO
SILENT HONOR	LOVE: POEMS
MALICE	THE RING
FIVE DAYS IN PARIS	LOVING
LIGHTNING	TO LOVE AGAIN
WINGS	SUMMER'S END
THE GIFT	SEASON OF PASSION
ACCIDENT	THE PROMISE
VANISHED	NOW AND FOREVER
MIXED BLESSINGS	GOLDEN MOMENTS*
JEWELS	GOING HOME
NO GREATER LOVE	

* Published outside the UK under the title PASSION'S PROMISE

DANIELLE STEEL

SUNSET IN ST TROPEZ

BANTAM PRESS

LONDON · NEW YORK · TORONTO · SYDNEY · AUCKLAND

TRANSWORLD PUBLISHERS
61–63 Uxbridge Road, London W5 5SA
a division of The Random House Group Ltd

RANDOM HOUSE AUSTRALIA (PTY) LTD
20 Alfred Street, Milsons Point, Sydney,
New South Wales 2061, Australia

RANDOM HOUSE NEW ZEALAND LTD
18 Poland Road, Glenfield, Auckland 10, New Zealand

RANDOM HOUSE SOUTH AFRICA (PTY) LTD
Endulini, 5a Jubilee Road, Parktown 2193, South Africa

Published 2002 by Bantam Press
a division of Transworld Publishers

Copyright © Danielle Steel 2002

The right of Danielle Steel to be identified
as the author of this work has been asserted in accordance
with sections 77 and 78 of the Copyright, Designs and
Patents Act 1988.

All the characters in this book
are fictitious, and any resemblance
to actual persons, living or dead,
is purely coincidental.

A catalogue record for this book is available
from the British Library.
ISBN 0593 048652

All rights reserved. No part of this publication may be reproduced,
stored in a retrieval system, or transmitted in any form or by any means,
electronic, mechanical, photocopying, recording, or otherwise, without
the prior permission of the publishers.

Typeset in 12/16.8pt Garamond by Falcon Oast Graphic Art Ltd.

Printed in Great Britain by
Clays Ltd, Bungay, Suffolk

1 3 5 7 9 10 8 6 4 2

To The Big Six:
Jerry and David,
Knud and Kirsten,
Beverly and John,
for always being there for me,
in good times, and bad times,
and great times,
beloved friends
of my heart.

         with all my love,
            d.s.

SUNSET IN ST TROPEZ

1

DIANA MORRISON LIT the candles in her dining room, on a table set for six. The apartment was large and elegant, with a view of Central Park. Diana and Eric had lived there for nineteen of the thirty-two years they'd been married, and for most of those years their two daughters had lived there with them. Both girls had moved out only in the last few years, Samantha to an apartment of her own when she graduated from Brown, and Katherine when she got married five years before. They were good girls, bright and loving and fun, and despite the expected skirmishes with them in their teens, Diana got along with them extremely well, and she missed them, now that they'd grown up.

But she and Eric had enjoyed their time alone. At fifty-five, she was still beautiful, and Eric had always been careful to keep the romance fresh between them. He heard enough stories through his work to understand what women needed from their men. At sixty, he was a handsome, youthful-looking man, and a year before he had talked Diana into getting her eyes done. He knew she would feel better if she did. And he'd been right, as she checked the table again that she had set for New Year's Eve, she looked glorious in the candlelight. The minor cosmetic surgery she'd had, had knocked ten years off her age.

She had let her hair go white years before, and it shimmered like fresh snow in a well-cut, angled bob that showed off her delicate features and big blue eyes. Eric always told her that she was as pretty as she'd been when they met. She'd been a nurse at Columbia-Presbyterian, when he was an obstetrical resident, and they'd gotten married six months later, and been together ever since. She'd stopped working when she got pregnant with Katherine, and stayed home after that, busy with the girls, and understanding with Eric as he got up night after night, to deliver babies. He loved his work, and she was proud of him.

He had one of the most successful ob/gyn practices in New York, and he said he wasn't tired of it yet, although two of his partners had retired the year before. But Eric still didn't mind the hours, and Diana was used to it by now. It didn't bother her when he left in the middle of the night, or had to cancel out of dinner parties at the last minute. They'd been living that way for more than thirty years. He worked on holidays and weekends, and loved what he did. He had been there with their daughter Katherine when both of her boys were born.

They were the perfect family in many ways, and life had been good to them. Theirs was an easy, fulfilling life, and a solid marriage. Diana kept busy now that the girls were grown, doing volunteer work at Sloan-Kettering, and organizing fund-raisers for research. She had no desire to go back to nursing once the girls grew up, and she knew she'd been out of it for too long. Besides, she had other interests now, her life had grown by leaps and bounds around her. Her charity work, the time she spent with Eric, their many interests, their trips, and her two grandsons filled her days.

As she stood in the dining room, she turned as she heard Eric walk into the living room, and for an instant, he stood in the doorway of the dining room, smiling at her, as their eyes met. The bond between them was evident, the solidity of their marriage rare.

"Good evening, Mrs. Morrison . . . you look incredible." His eyes said it even before his words did. It was always easy to see, and to know, how much he loved her. He had a handsome, boyish face, strong features, a cleft chin, eyes the same bright blue as her own, and his hair had drifted effortlessly from sandy blond to gray. He looked particularly handsome in his dinner jacket, he was trim, and in good shape, with the same narrow waist and broad shoulders he had had when they got married. He rode a bike in the park on Sunday afternoons, and played tennis whenever he wasn't on call on the weekend. And he either played squash or swam, no matter how tired he was, every night when he finished at the office. The two of them looked like an ad for healthy, attractive middle-aged people. "Happy New Year, sweetheart," he added as he walked over, put an arm around her, and kissed her. "What time are they coming?" "They" referred to the two couples who were their favorite companions and best friends.

"At eight," she said, as she checked the champagne cooling in a silver bucket, and he poured himself a martini. "Or at least Robert and Anne will. Pascale and John should be here sometime before midnight." He laughed as he dropped an extra olive in his glass and glanced at Diana.

Eric and John Donnally had gone to Harvard together, and been friends ever since. They were as different as night and day. Eric was tall and lean, easygoing, open, and generous of spirit. He loved women, and as he did every day in his practice, he could spend hours talking to them. John was stocky, powerful, irascible, ornery, argued constantly with his wife, and pretended to have a roving eye, although no one had ever actually seen him do anything about it. And in truth, John loved his wife, although he would rather have died than admit it publicly, even among his closest friends. Listening to him and Pascale talk was like hearing a series of rapid-fire explosions. She was as volatile as he was, and eight years younger than Diana. Pascale was French and had been dancing with the New York City Ballet when John met her. She was twenty-two years old when they met, and twenty-five years later, she was as tiny and graceful as she had been then, with big green eyes, dark brown hair, and an incredible figure. She had been teaching ballet for the past ten years, in her spare time. There were only two obvious things that were similar about Pascale and John—neither one was ever punctual— and both had difficult dispositions, and loved to argue, for hours on end. They had turned the art of bickering into an Olympic sport.

The last of Eric and Diana's guests for New Year's Eve were Robert and Anne Smith. They had met the Morrisons thirty years before when Eric delivered Anne's first baby, and their friendship with the Morrisons was born at the same time. Anne and Robert were both attorneys. She was still practicing, at sixty-one, and Robert had become a superior court judge. At sixty-three, he had the appropriately solemn looks that went with his position. But his sometimes dour demeanor was a mask for a kind and gentle heart. He loved his wife, his children, and his friends. He was tall and good looking, and deeply devoted to Anne, and their three children. Eric had delivered all three, and had become one of Anne's favorite friends.

Robert and Anne had married in law school, and had

been together for thirty-eight years. They were the elder statesmen of the group, seemed the most staid, mostly because of their jobs. But they were warm and lively among friends, and had their own style, as the others did as well. They weren't as colorful or as excitable as Pascale and John, or as youthful and stylish in their looks as Eric and Diana. Robert and Anne looked their age, but were young at heart. The six friends were deeply attached to each other, and always had a good time together. They saw a lot of each other, more so than other friends.

They had dinner once or twice a month, and had shared their joys and hopes and disappointments over the years, their concerns about their children, and even Pascale's deep grief when she was never able to have children. She had wanted them desperately once she retired from the ballet, but it had never worked out for her, and even the fertility specialists Eric sent her to had been unable to do anything for them. Half a dozen attempts at in vitro, and even donor eggs, had been fruitless. And John had stubbornly refused to even consider adopting. He didn't want "someone else's juvenile delinquent," he wanted his own, or none at all. So at forty-seven and sixty, they were childless, and had only each other to rail at, which they both did often, on a variety of subjects, most of the time much to the amusement of the others, who were accustomed to the heated arguments Pascale and John made no attempt to hide and seemed to enjoy.

The three couples had chartered a sailboat in the Caribbean together once, and rented a house in Long Island several times. They had gone to Europe together more than once, and always enjoyed their joint travels. Despite their very different styles, they were totally compatible, and the best of friends. They not only tolerated each other's foibles, but understood each other in important ways. They had shared a lot of history with each other over time.

It was fitting that they spend New Year's Eve together. And for the past two decades, it had been a tradition that all three couples cherished, and counted on every year. They rotated houses from year to year, going to Robert and Anne's for quiet, early evenings some years, which ended just after the stroke of midnight, or to John and Pascale's, for disorganized, hastily thrown together, but delicious dinners, and the champagne and wines John and Pascale argued about and collected. She preferred French wines, and he opted for California. But everyone's favorite locale for New Year's Eve was Eric and Diana's. Their home was comfortable and elegant, the cook Diana used for evenings like these was excellent and capable, and never intruded, the food was good, the wines were great, and in their impeccably decorated apartment, everyone felt they had to look their best and be on their best behavior. Even Pascale and John made an effort to behave when they came there, although they didn't always succeed, and some minor argument would erupt about the name of a wine neither of them could remember, or a trip they wanted to take. John loved Africa, and Pascale the South of France, and often John would make inflammatory comments about Pascale's mother, whom he hated. He pretended to hate France, the French, and everything about them, including and most especially his mother-in-law, and Pascale would cheerfully reciprocate, with acerbic comments about his mother in Boston. But despite their quirks and vagaries, there was no doubt about the fact that the six friends were far more than fond of each other. Theirs was a deep bond of affection, which had withstood the test of time, and no matter how often or seldom it was, they looked forward to seeing each other. And best of all, whenever they were together, all six of them had a good time.

The doorbell rang at exactly seven-fifty-nine, and neither Eric nor Diana was surprised when she opened the door, and found Anne in a high-necked black evening gown with discreet pearl earrings, her gray hair combed into a bun, and Robert in a tuxedo, with perfectly groomed snow-white hair, standing on the doorstep, smiling at them.

"Good evening," Robert said with a twinkle in his eye as he bent from his considerable height to kiss Diana, and the foursome wished each other a happy New Year. "Are we late?" Robert asked, looking concerned. Robert was punctual to a fault, as was Anne. "The traffic was awful." They lived in the East Eighties, whereas Pascale and John had to come from their apartment near Lincoln Center, on the West Side. But God only knew when they would get there. And to complicate matters further, it had started snowing, which would make it hard to find a cab.

Anne took off her wrap, and smiled at Diana. Although she was only six years older than Diana, Anne looked like her mother. She had warm brown eyes, and wore her silvery-gray hair in a bun. She was a pretty woman, but had never concentrated on her looks. She wore almost no makeup, and had exquisite creamy skin. She preferred to spend her time on art, theater, obscure books, and music, when she wasn't busy with her family practice law firm. She was an advocate for children's rights, and had spent huge amounts of time in recent years, helping to set up programs for abused women. It was a labor of love for which she had received numerous awards. She and Robert shared their passion for the law, the plight of children and the abused, and both were well known for espousing liberal causes. Anne had thought long and hard about going into politics years before, and had been encouraged to do so, but had decided against it, for the sake of her husband and children. She preferred private to public life, and had no desire for the attention it would have focused on her. In spite of her considerable professional abilities, she was an admirably unassuming person, to the point of being humble, and Robert was proud of her. He was one of her most vocal fans.

As Anne sat down in the living room, Eric sat down next to her on the couch and put an arm around her. "So where have you been for the past two weeks? I feel like we haven't seen you in ages." Robert and Anne had spent the holidays in Vermont, as they always did, with their children and grandchildren. They had two married sons, and a single daughter, who had only recently finished law school. But no matter where Anne and Robert were, or what they did, they always came back to spend New Year's Eve with their friends. They had missed only one year, when Anne's father had died and she had to go to Chicago, to be with her mother. But other than that, this was a sacred engagement every year, for all six of them.

"We were in Sugarbush, changing diapers and looking for lost mittens," Anne explained to Eric with a smile. She had a kind face, and laughing eyes. They had five grandchildren, and two daughters-in-law whom Diana had always sensed Anne didn't like, although she would never have said it out loud. Neither of her daughters-in-law worked, and Anne didn't approve of the extent to which her sons indulged them. She thought women should work too. She always had. And in the privacy of their own home, Anne had said to Robert repeatedly that she thought their daughters-in-law were spoiled. "How were the holidays for you?" Anne smiled up at her old friend as she asked. Eric was like a brother to her, and had been for years.

"Nice, we had a great time with Katherine and Sam. One of Kathy's boys knocked over the tree, or tried to at least, and the little one stuck a peanut up his nose, and I had to take him to the emergency room on Christmas Eve to remove it."

"That sounds about right, one of Jeff's kids broke his arm in ski school," Anne said with a look of concern, and relief to have left them with their parents. She enjoyed her grandchildren but readily admitted they wore her out, and Robert agreed. He loved his children and grandchildren and spending time with them, but he equally enjoyed spending time alone with Anne. Their marriage had been a quiet but powerful love affair throughout the years. He was crazy about her.

"It makes you wonder how any of our children survived their childhood," Diana said, as she handed Anne a glass of champagne and sat down to join her, as Robert stood sipping his champagne with a look of admiration at his wife. He had told her how beautiful she looked and kissed her before they left their house.

"I don't know why, but I think things were easier when our kids were younger," Anne sighed with a smile, "or maybe that was just because I was at the office when the kids were small." Anne smiled at Robert. Despite their family, and their jobs, they had always made time for each other and romance. "Everything seems more stressful these days, or maybe my nerves just aren't what they used to be with young kids around, although I love them. But it's so nice to have a quiet civilized evening, with grown-ups." She looked at the Morrisons with pleasure. "The decibel level at the house in Sugarbush nearly drove Robert crazy." They had admitted to each other in the car that they were delighted to come home.

"I'm going to enjoy my grandchildren a lot more when I start to lose my hearing," he said, setting his glass down on the coffee table, as the doorbell rang. It was nearly eight-thirty, a record in punctuality for the Donnallys, who typically would arrive late, and blame each other for it, each one insisting vehemently that it was the other's fault. And tonight was no different.

Eric opened the door to them as Diana chatted with the Smiths, and a moment later, they could all hear Pascale and John.

"I'm so sorry we're late," Pascale said in her still heavily accented English, although she had lived in New York for nearly thirty years, and spoke the language flawlessly. But she had never been able to shake her French accent, or tried to. She still preferred to speak French whenever possible, with people she met, sales personnel in stores, waiters, and several times a week on the phone with her mother. John claimed they spent hours on the phone. And for all twenty-five years of their marriage, John had steadfastly refused to learn French, although he caught key words here and there, and could say *"Merde"* with a fairly credible accent. "John absolutely *refused* to find a cab!" Pascale said in outraged disbelief as Eric took her coat with a familiar grin. He always loved their stories. "He *forced* me to take the bus here! Can you imagine? On New Year's Eve, in evening clothes!" She looked incensed as she brushed a lock of curly dark hair from her eyes, the rest was pulled back in a tight bun, just as she had worn it when she was dancing, only now the front was softer. And in spite of her forty-seven years, there was still something overwhelmingly sensual and exquisite about her. She was tiny and delicate and graceful, and her green eyes were blazing as she told her tale of woe to Eric.

"I didn't *refuse* to take a cab—we couldn't *find* one!" John said, defending himself, as Pascale groaned at him.

"Ahh!" she said, sparks darting from her eyes, as she glared at her husband. "Ridiculous! You just didn't want to pay the cab fare!" John was notoriously parsimonious among all those who knew him. But with the snow falling steadily, it was entirely possible, in this instance at least, that they hadn't been able to find a taxi. And for once John looked singularly undisturbed by his wife's attack, as they walked into the living room with Eric, to find the others. John was in excellent humor as he greeted their friends.

"Sorry we're late," he said calmly. He was used to his wife's inflammatory outbursts, and generally undismayed by them. She was French, easily offended, and frequently outraged. John was, as a rule, a great deal calmer, at least at the outset. It took him just a little longer to respond and heat up. He was stocky and powerful, and had played ice hockey at Harvard. And he and Pascale made an interesting visual of contrasts, the one so delicate and petite, the other strong and broad-shouldered and powerful. Everyone had commented for years on how much they looked like Katharine Hepburn and Spencer Tracy. "Happy New Year, everyone," John said, smiling broadly, as he accepted a flute of champagne from Diana, while Pascale kissed Eric on both cheeks, and then did the same to Anne and Robert, and a moment later Diana hugged her and told her how lovely she looked. Pascale always did. She had exquisite, exotic looks.

"Alors, les copains," she said, calling them the equivalent of "buddies," "how was Christmas? Ours was awful," she volunteered without stopping for breath. "John hated the suit I bought him, and he bought me a stove, can you imagine! A *stove*! Why not a lawn mower, or a truck!" She looked incensed as the others laughed, and her husband was quick to answer in his own defense.

"I wouldn't buy you any kind of vehicle, Pascale, you're a lousy driver!" But he said it, this time at least, with good humor.

"I'm a much better driver than you are," she said, sipping the champagne, "and you know it. You're even afraid to drive in Paris."

"I'm not afraid of anything in France, except your mother." She rolled her eyes, and turned her attention to Robert. He always enjoyed talking to her. He had a passion for classical ballet, as did Anne, and good theater. And he and Pascale talked about ballet sometimes for hours. He also enjoyed practicing his rusty French on her, which pleased Pascale immensely.

The group chatted amiably till dinnertime, drinking champagne, and talking and laughing. John conceded finally that he was pleased to have taken the bus, to have been spared the price of a cab, and everyone teased him about it. He was famous in their midst for his distaste for spending money, and they loved to tease him about it. He was the butt of endless jokes, and loved them all.

Eric and Anne talked about the skiing in Sugarbush, and Diana chimed in that she was dying to go back to Aspen. Pascale and Robert chatted about the opening of the ballet. And Diana and John talked about the state of the economy, the stock market, and some of the Morrisons' investments. John was an investment banker, and he loved talking business with anyone who'd indulge him. The interests of the group had always meshed well, and they moved easily from serious subjects to light ones. And as Diana told them they were ready to sit down to dinner in the dining room, Anne mentioned to Eric that her elder son and daughter-in-law were having another baby. It would be their sixth grandchild.

"At least I will never be traumatized by having someone call me Grandma," Pascale said lightly, but they all knew that to Pascale there was more sorrow to it than her casual comment suggested. They all remembered the half-dozen years when she had reported to all of them regularly about her intensive treatments, the medicines she took, the shots John had to give her several times a day, and her ongoing failure to get pregnant. The group had been unfailingly supportive of them, to no avail. It had been a terrible time for them, and one that they all had feared would ultimately cost them their marriage, but fortunately, it hadn't.

The real tragedy for Pascale had come when John absolutely refused to adopt a baby. For Pascale, it was the final sentence meted out to her that she would never have a child, which, at the time at least, had been all she wanted. In recent years, she claimed that she no longer thought about it. But she looked wistful still sometimes when the others talked about their children. Eric had even tried talking to John, to convince him to adopt, but he had been intransigent about it. John was nothing if not stubborn, and no matter how much it meant to Pascale, he refused to consider it as an option for them. He did *not* want to bring up, support, or attempt to love someone else's baby. He was very clear about the fact that he felt he couldn't, even for her sake. And the others in the group had been deeply sorry for them.

But there was no talk of it now as they moved to the elegantly set table. Diana set the prettiest tables of them all, and did the most exotic flower arrangements. Tonight she had mixed birds-of-paradise with cymbidium orchids, and there were little silver bells spread all over the table, handsome silver candlesticks with tall white candles in them, and the embroidered tablecloth she'd used had been her mother's and was spectacular. The table looked superb.

"I don't know how you do it," Anne said admiringly, taking in the magic Diana had created, as she stood by looking as elegant as her table in a white satin gown that was the same color as her hair and showed off her youthful figure. She was in almost as good shape as Pascale, though not quite, since Pascale danced for six hours every day, with her students. Anne hadn't been as blessed as either of the other two women. She was attractive, but she was tall, and bigger boned than either of the other two, and now and then she complained that they made her feel like an Amazon beside them. But it didn't really bother her, she was brilliant, fun to be with, self-assured, and it was obvious even to her how much Robert loved her. He had told her frequently over the years that she was the most beautiful woman he'd ever seen, and he meant it.

Eric put an arm around Diana and kissed her before they sat down at the dinner table, and thanked her for what a beautiful job she'd done, as Pascale glowered across the table at John.

"If you did that to me, I'd have a heart attack from shock," she scolded him. "You never kiss me, and you never thank me. For *anything*!" But despite her frequent complaints, there was no malice in Pascale's tone.

"Thank you, darling," John smiled benevolently at her from his seat, "for all those wonderful frozen dinners you leave me." He laughed in a good-natured way as he said it. She often went to dance class at night, after teaching all day, and didn't have time to cook him dinner.

"How can you say that? I left you a cassoulet last week, and a coq au vin two days ago. . . . You don't deserve them!!"

"No, I don't. Besides, I cook better than you do." He laughed at her.

"You're a monster!" she said, green eyes blazing at him. "And I'm not taking the bus home. I'm taking a taxi home by myself, John Donnally, and I will not allow you to ride with me!" She looked unfailingly, incredibly French. Theirs had always been a match of fire and passion.

"I was hoping you'd say that," he said, grinning at Diana, as she served their first course of bluepoint oysters. The six of them shared a particular fondness for seafood.

She had cold lobster for the main course, then salad and cheese, in deference to Pascale, who couldn't bear to eat salad first, and always said she felt cheated when there wasn't cheese after the main course. And there was baked Alaska for dessert, which was Eric's favorite, and the others loved it too. It was a festive meal, and a perfect evening for all six of them.

"My God, we eat well at your house," John said admiringly as Diana came out of the kitchen with the flaming dessert, and the assembled company applauded. "Pascale, why don't you borrow some of Diana's recipes instead of all those guts and entrails and brains and kidneys and blood sausages you feed me?"

"You wouldn't let me spend the money if I did," Pascale said truthfully. "Besides, you love brains and kidneys," she said matter-of-factly.

"I lied. I'd rather eat lobster," he said, beaming at his hostess, as Robert chuckled. The constant bickering and bantering of the Donnallys somehow amused him, even after twenty-five years of listening to it. To all of them, it seemed harmless. Their marriages were all sound, their mates reliable and constant, and their relationships surprisingly harmonious in a world that offered little harmony to most people. They all realized that they'd been blessed, not only in their mates, but in their bond of friendship to each other. Robert called them the six musketeers, and although their interests were varied and different sometimes, they nevertheless enjoyed the time they spent together.

It was after eleven o'clock when Anne commented on the fact that both John and Eric had turned sixty that year, and it no longer made her feel quite as ancient, since she was a year older, and had hated turning sixty the year before.

"We should do something to celebrate it," Diana said, as they sat over coffee and John lit a cigar, since none of the others objected. It was a taste that Pascale shared with him, and occasionally she smoked one with him. It had become fashionable for women to do that in recent years, but Pascale always had, ever since they'd been married. It seemed incongruous in light of her delicate appearance.

"What do you suggest to celebrate our turning sixty?" Eric asked his wife, with a grin. "Face-lifts for all of us? The men at least, none of you ladies need it," he said, looking admiringly at his wife. It was the one secret she hadn't shared with her friends, the fact that she'd had her eyes done, at Eric's suggestion. He had found her the surgeon. "I think John would look great, if he had some work done." In truth, he had a few wrinkles and lines, but they looked well on him. He had a manly air that suited his personality perfectly.

"Better liposuction for him," Pascale said, looking at

her husband through the smoke, and he looked undismayed by the comment.

"It's those damn blood sausages you feed me," he accused her.

"And if I stopped making them for you?" she challenged.

"I'd kill you," he grinned, and handed her the cigar to take a puff, which she did, with a look of pleasure. For all their teasing and bantering, she and John genuinely liked each other.

"I'm serious," Diana persisted. They had another half-hour until midnight. "We should celebrate our men coming of age." Only she and Pascale were still several years from that landmark, although Diana was closer to it than Pascale, and she wasn't looking forward to it. "Why don't we take another trip together?"

"Where do you suggest?" Robert asked, with a look of interest. When they could get away from their demanding professional lives, he and Anne both enjoyed traveling to exotic places. The summer before they had gone to Bali and Indonesia. It was a trip they would remember forever.

"What about a safari in Kenya?" John asked hopefully, and Pascale looked at him with disgust. She had gone to Botswana with him years before, to a game preserve, and hated every minute of it. The only place she ever wanted to go was Paris, to see friends and relatives, but John didn't consider that a vacation. It drove him crazy to stay with her family, and visit her relatives with her, while she chatted endlessly in French, and he understood nothing of what they were saying, and didn't want to. He adored Pascale, but her relatives either annoyed or bored him.

"I hate Africa, and bugs and dirt. Why don't we all go to Paris together?" Pascale asked with a look of pleasure. As much as John hated it, she loved it.

"What a great idea," he said, drawing on the cigar again, having just relit it. "Let's all stay with your mother. I'm sure she'd love it. We could all stand in line for a couple of hours, waiting for your grandmother to get out of the bathroom." Like most Paris flats, they only had one, and Pascale's ninety-two-year-old grandmother lived with her widowed aunt and mother. It was an atmosphere that drove John insane, and to a lot of bourbon, whenever he stayed there. The last time he had even brought his own, since the most exotic thing in her mother's bar was Dubonnet and sweet vermouth, although there was always excellent red wine with dinner. Her late father had been a connoisseur of fine wines, and Pascale's mother had learned a great deal from him. It was the only thing John liked about her.

"Don't be rude about my grandmother. And your mother is even more impossible than mine," Pascale said, looking very Gallic and highly insulted.

"At least mine speaks English."

"You wouldn't want to stay with my mother either," Diana volunteered, and the others laughed. They had all met Diana's parents several times, and although her father was a pleasant man, Diana made no secret of the fact that her highly organized, extremely domineering mother had always driven her crazy. "Seriously, where could we go together? What about the Caribbean? Or someplace really exotic this time? Like Buenos Aires, or Rio?"

"Everyone says Rio is dangerous," Anne said with a look of concern. "My cousin went there last year, and they stole her handbag, her luggage, and her passport. She said she'd never go back there. What about Mexico?"

"Or Japan or Mainland China," Robert suggested, beginning to warm up to the idea. He liked traveling with the others, and he had a particular fondness for Asia. "Or Hong Kong. The girls could go shopping."

"What's wrong with France?" Pascale tried again, and the others laughed, as John pretended to slump in his chair in despair. They went there every summer. "I'm serious. Why don't we rent a house in the South of France? Aix en Provence, or Antibes, or Eze . . . or what about St Tropez? It's terrific." John instantly objected, but as he did, Diana looked intrigued at the prospect.

"Actually, why not? It might be fun to rent a house, and maybe someone Pascale knows could find us a good one. It might be more fun than traveling around some exotic country. Eric and I speak enough French to get by,

Anne is pretty good at it, and so is Robert. Pascale can handle all the hard stuff. What do you think, guys?"

Anne looked pensive as she considered it, and nodded. "To tell you the truth, I like it. Robert and I went to St Tropez with the kids ten years ago, and we loved it. It's pretty, on the water, the food is great, and it's very lively." She and Robert had spent a romantic week there, in spite of their children.

"We could rent a house there for August. And John," Diana promised him with an earnest look, "we won't let Pascale's mother come near it."

"Actually, we might get lucky. She goes to Italy every year in August."

"See, it would be perfect. What do you all think?" Diana asked, pressing the project through, even Robert was nodding his approval. St Tropez had a nice ring to it, it was civilized and fun, and they could charter a boat to visit other places on the Riviera.

"I like it," Robert admitted, and Eric seconded the motion.

"I vote for St Tropez," he said solemnly, "if we can find a decent house. Pascale, what do you think? Can you handle that end of the project for us?"

"No problem. I know some very good real estate agents in Paris. And if she can leave my grandmother, my mother could look at some for us."

"No," John said emphatically, "keep her out of it. She'll

pick something we hate. Just go with the agent." But he didn't object to the location, even though it was in what he usually referred to as Frogland.

"Is it unanimous then?" Diana inquired, looking around the table, and everyone nodded. "Then it's St Tropez in August."

Pascale was beaming as Diana said it. There was nothing in the world that appealed to her more than a month in the South of France with their best friends, and even John looked somewhat resigned to it as Eric announced that it was midnight.

"Happy New Year, sweetheart," Eric said, kissing his wife, as Robert leaned toward Anne, kissed her discreetly on the lips, and put his arms around her as he wished her good things in the coming year, as Pascale came around the table to kiss her husband. He was surrounded by a cloud of smoke from the cigar, but she didn't mind the taste of it, as he kissed her on the mouth with slightly more passion than she had expected. For all their battles and the noise they made, theirs was as solid a marriage as the others', in some ways even more so, as all they had as their bond was each other, and no children to distract them.

"I can't wait till next summer in St Tropez," Pascale said breathlessly as she came up for air. "It's going to be fantastic."

"If it isn't," John said practically, "we'll have to kill you,

Pascale, since it was your idea. Just make sure you find us a decent house. No summer rat trap that they foist off on unsuspecting tourists."

"I'll find the best house in St Tropez, I promise," she vowed to all of them, as she took the cigar from John again, and drew on it, as she perched on his lap, and everyone talked animatedly about the plans they'd made. The one thing they all agreed on easily was that it was going to be a terrific summer. Coming up with the idea had been a wonderful way to usher in the New Year.

2

THE NEXT TIME they all got together was at Pascale and John's West Side apartment, two weeks later, on a night when it was pouring rain. The Morrisons and Smiths arrived punctually, as always, and left their dripping raincoats and umbrellas in the Donnallys' front hall. The decor at the Donnallys' was eclectic, there were African masks, modern sculptures, antiques Pascale had brought from France, and beautiful Persian rugs. And there were fascinating objects she had bought on her travels with the ballet.

The light was soft and the aroma from the kitchen delicious. She had made thick mushroom soup, and rabbit in mustard sauce for the main course. And John had opened several bottles of Haut-Brion.

"It smells wonderful!" Anne said, warming her hands at the fire John had lit, as Pascale passed a plate of hors d'oeuvres.

"Don't believe everything you smell!" John warned, pouring them each a glass of champagne. "You-know-who made dinner!" he said with a grin of warning.

"Toi alors!" Pascale said with an evil glare at him, before disappearing into the kitchen to check on dinner again. But she had good news for all of them, she said, when she came back to sit down with them on the dark red velvet couches in their living room. There was a handsome painting over the fireplace, and candles lit everywhere, and on one wall were dozens of photographs of Pascale with the New York City Ballet. It was a room that reflected both their personalities, the places they had been, and the life they led. And the aura of the room was definitely French. There was even an open pack of Gauloises on the table, which Pascale indulged in from time to time, while John smoked his cigars.

"So what have you been up to?" Diana asked, as she leaned back against the couch, in a well-tailored black pantsuit, sipping her champagne. She had been hard at work all day, organizing another fund-raiser at Sloan-Kettering. And Eric had been up for three nights in a row, delivering babies. The whole group seemed quieter than usual, and a little tired.

"I found a house!" Pascale beamed, as she went to the handsome old partners' desk she and John had found in London years before. She returned with a thick manila envelope, and handed a stack of photographs to her friends. *"Voilà!* It's exactly what we wanted." John reserved comment for once, he had already seen the photographs, and although he didn't like the price, he had to admit he liked the house. It was an elegant, well-maintained, rambling old villa, with beautiful gardens and lovely grounds. It was right on the water, there was a small dock, and a pretty little sailboat came with it, which would be fun for all of them, particularly Eric and Robert and Anne, who were the sailors of the group. And the photographs of the interior showed a handsome living room filled with French provincial furniture, five huge well-decorated bedrooms, and a dining room big enough to seat two dozen people. The kitchen was immaculate, though a little old-fashioned, but it was cozy and had a lot of charm. And best of all, there was both a maid and a gardener, who was willing to act as chauffeur. Pascale was right, they all agreed, it looked like the perfect house. In fact, it was called Coup de Foudre, which meant "love at first sight," or "bolt of lightning." It was available for the entire month of August, and quite reasonably, because of the desirability of the house, the owners wanted to know immediately if they were going to rent it.

"Wow, that looks great, Pascale," Diana said with pleasure, poring over the pictures again. "It even has two guest rooms, if we want to invite friends, or some of our kids. And I love the idea of the maid. I don't mind cooking, but I hate cleaning up after."

"Exactly," Pascale said, looking thrilled that they liked it. "It's a little expensive," she admitted hesitantly, "but divided by three, it's not so bad." John rolled his eyes at that, but even he had to admit that it wasn't beyond reason. He was going to use air miles to cover the air fare, and if the girls did most of the cooking, and they didn't go out to fashionable restaurants every night, it almost sounded reasonable to him.

"Do you suppose it really is as good as it looks in the pictures?" Robert asked cautiously, helping himself to Pascale's hors d'oeuvres. Her culinary skills were a lot better than John admitted. Most of the pretty little canapés had already been devoured, and the aroma wafting from the kitchen smelled delicious.

"Why would they lie to us?" Pascale asked, looking surprised. It was the same thing John had said. "I used a very reputable agent to find it. I can ask my mother to fly down to see it, if you want."

"Oh God, no!" John said, looking horrified. "Don't let her get involved in this. She'll tell them I'm a rich American banker, and they'll double the price." He looked agonized just thinking of it, and the others laughed at him.

"I think it looks absolutely perfect," Anne said sensibly. She had been enthusiastic about the project from the beginning. "I think we ought to move on it before we lose it to someone else. And even if it turns out to be a little less perfect than the pictures, so what? How bad can a month be in a villa in the South of France? I vote that we fax them tonight and tell them we want it," she said decisively, with a warm smile to Pascale. "You did a great job!"

"Thank you," Pascale said, looking ecstatic. She loved the idea of spending an additional month in France. She always stayed with her family in Paris for most of June, and all of July. But this year she could also stay for August.

"I agree with Anne," Robert said without hesitation. "And I like the idea of the guest rooms. I know our kids would love to come over for a few days, if the rest of you don't mind."

"I'll bet ours would too," Eric joined in, and Diana nodded.

"I don't know if Katherine's husband could get away, but I know she'd love to come over with the boys, and Samantha is crazy about France."

"So am I," Anne smiled. "Do we agree then? Shall we do it?" They rapidly calculated how much it would cost each couple, and although John pretended to clutch his heart as they converted it to dollars, in the end they all agreed that for a house as large and well cared for as this one, it was a fair price, and well worth doing.

"It's a done deal then," Robert said, looking pleased. He knew he could arrange to take the month off, and he wanted Anne to take a vacation. She had been looking

31

very tired, and even she admitted that she worked too hard. Robert had even told her lately that he thought she should think about retiring. Life was too short to spend every waking hour either in the office, in the courtroom, or preparing cases for their litigators to try. Although she loved her work, it was very stressful, and her clients demanded a lot of her. She worked nights and some weekends, and although her career was her passion, he was beginning to think it was time for her to slow down. He wanted to spend more time with her. "Will you take the whole month off?" he asked his wife pointedly as Pascale called them in to dinner, and Anne nodded, with a twinkle in her eye. "Do you mean that? I'm going to hold you to it, you know," he said, as he pulled her close to him and kissed her. He was really looking forward to their time together in France. For the past two years, she had cut short their vacations in order to come back to the office and handle emergencies for her clients.

"I promise to stay for the whole time," she said solemnly, and meant it. For now at least.

"Then it's worth every penny," Robert said, looking happy as they walked into the dining room arm in arm. They looked very distinguished together, and very cozy.

"Particularly with a sailboat," she teased him. Sailing with him was one of her great pleasures, and it always reminded them of their early summers on Cape Cod, when the children were small.

All six of them talked animatedly about the house in St Tropez all night. It was a lively, friendly evening. They talked briefly as well about their work and their children, but for the most part, they talked about the villa and the time they were planning in France.

And as they sat drinking Château d'Yquem afterward, at the dining table, they felt the warm glow of the pleasure they had in store for them. It sounded like a perfect summer to all of them.

"I can even go down a few days before, if they let me, to get things organized and buy whatever we need for the house," Pascale volunteered, although there wouldn't be much to add, the brochure said that the house came fully equipped with bed linens, towels, everything they needed in the kitchen, and Eric said he was sure that the couple who came with the house would probably have everything well in hand. "I don't mind going down before you all arrive," Pascale said cheerfully, and even her husband smiled. They had come up with a very appealing plan.

It was nearly midnight when they finally disbanded, and the Morrisons and Smiths shared a cab to the East Side. It was still raining, but they were in high spirits, as Anne leaned back against the seat in the cab and smiled at them. Robert suspected that he was the only one who noticed how tired she looked. She seemed exhausted.

"Are you okay?" Robert asked her gently after they dropped off the Morrisons. Anne had been quieter than usual in the cab, and he could see that she was tired. She had been pushing herself too hard again.

"I'm absolutely fine," she said with less energy than conviction, "I was just thinking about how nice it's going to be to spend a month in France. I can't think of anything I'd rather do with you than have time like that, reading, relaxing, sailing, swimming. I just wish it weren't such a long time from now." It seemed a long time to wait for their next vacation.

"So do I," Robert echoed. The cab dropped them off in front of their house on East Eighty-ninth Street, and they rushed inside to get out of the rain, and as Robert watched Anne take off her coat in their comfortable apartment, he thought she looked pale. "I wish you'd take some time off before next summer. Why don't we take a long weekend, and go someplace warm for a few days?" He worried about her, he always had. She was the most precious person in his life. Even more than his children, Anne had always been his top priority. She was his lover, his confidante, his ally, his best friend. She was the hub of his existence.

When she'd been pregnant, and for the few times she'd been ill in their thirty-eight years together, he had treated her like antique glass. He was, by nature, a very nurturing person. She loved that about him, his tenderness, his caring, his gentle spirit. She had seen that in him the first time she met him, and the years since had proven her right. In some ways, she was hardier than he was, tougher, stronger, and in some ways less forgiving. She was fierce when defending her clients' rights, or her children, but it was Robert who had always owned her heart. She didn't say it to him often, but theirs was a bond that had withstood the test of time, and needed few words. When they were younger, they used to talk more, about their hopes, their dreams, and how they felt. It was Robert who was the romantic, the dreamer who envisioned what the years ahead would be like. Anne was always more practical, and more wrapped up in their daily life. And as the years went on, there seemed to be less to talk about, less need to plan and look ahead. They just moved along, hand in hand, from year to year, satisfied with what they'd done, respectful of the lessons they'd learned. The only tragedy they had shared had been the loss of a fourth child, another daughter, at birth. It had devastated Anne at the time, but she had recovered quickly, thanks to Robert's support and kindness. It was Robert who had mourned the little girl for years, and who still talked about her from time to time. Anne had put it behind her, and instead of grieving for what she had lost, she was satisfied with what she had. But knowing how deeply Robert felt things, she was careful with his emotions, and unfailingly kind. He was the sort of person you wanted to shield from things that hurt him. Anne always seemed just a little better able than he was to take the blows that life dealt.

"What do you want to do tomorrow?" he asked as she slipped into bed beside him in a blue flannel nightgown. She was a handsome woman, not beautiful, but distinguished, elegant, and fine. And in some ways, he thought her even more attractive than he had when they were first married. She had the kind of looks that improved with time. She had worn well as his lifetime companion.

"Tomorrow, I want to sleep late, and read the paper," she answered with a yawn. "Do you want to go to a movie tomorrow afternoon?" They liked going to the movies, usually foreign films, or serious ones, which more often than not made Robert cry. When they were younger, she used to tease him about it. Anne never cried in movies. But she loved his tenderness and soft heart.

"That sounds like fun." They had a good time together, they enjoyed the same people, the same music and books, most of the same things, even more so now than in their early years. In the beginning, there had been more differences between them, but Robert had shared so much with her that over time, their tastes had merged, and their differences disappeared. What they shared now was intensely comfortable, like a huge feather bed into which they sank, hand in hand, with total ease.

"I'm glad Pascale found that house," Anne said as she drifted off to sleep, cuddled up to him. "I think next summer is really going to be fun."

"I can't wait to spend some time sailing with you," he said, as he pulled her close to him. He had felt amorous toward her earlier that night, while they got dressed to go to the Donnallys', but she was so tired now, it would have seemed unfair to try and make love to her. She worked too hard, and pushed herself too much. He made a mental note to lecture her about it the next day, he hadn't seen her this tired in years. And as he held her in his arms, she fell asleep almost instantly, and a few minutes later, he was asleep too, snoring softly.

It was four o'clock in the morning when he woke up, and heard Anne in the bathroom, she was coughing, and it sounded as though she was throwing up. He could see the light under the bathroom door, and he waited a few minutes to see if she came back to bed. But ten minutes later, there was no sound, and she still hadn't emerged from the bathroom. He got up finally, and knocked on the door, but she didn't answer.

"Anne, are you okay?" He was waiting to hear her say that she was fine and for him to go back to bed, but there was no sound from within. "Anne? Sweetheart . . . are you sick?" The dinner Pascale had prepared had been delicious, but heavy and rich. He waited another minute or two, and then gently turned the knob and peeked in, and what he saw was his wife, lying on the floor, her hair disheveled, her nightgown askew. There was evidence that she'd been vomiting, she was unconscious, and her face was gray, her lips almost blue. The sight of her terrified him. "Oh my God . . . oh my God . . ." He checked her pulse, and he could still feel it, but he couldn't see her breathe. He wasn't sure whether to try to revive her, or call 911. And in the end, he ran for his cellular phone, returned to Anne rapidly, and called from the bathroom. He had tried to shake her, call her name, but Anne showed no sign of regaining consciousness, and Robert could see that her lips were turning a deep blue. The 911 operator was already on the phone by then, and he gave his name and address and told them his wife was unconscious and barely breathing.

"Did she hit her head?" the operator said in a businesslike tone, as Robert fought back tears of terror and frustration.

"I don't know . . . do something . . . please . . . send someone right away. . . ." He put his cheek close to her nose, still holding the phone, but he could feel no breath on his face, and this time when he felt for her pulse, at first he thought it was gone, and then he picked it up again, but he could hardly feel it. It was as though she were rapidly slipping away from him, and he could do nothing to stop it. "Please . . . please help me . . . I think she's dying. . . ."

"There's an ambulance on the way," the voice said reassuringly, "but I need some more information from you. How old is your wife?"

"Sixty-one."

"Does she have a history of heart disease?"

"No, she was tired, very, very tired, and she's overworked," and then without saying more, he put down the phone, and gave her mouth-to-mouth resuscitation, he could hear her breath catch and she let out a sigh, but there was no other sign of life from her. She was as gray as she had been before, as Robert picked up his phone again. "I don't know what's wrong with her, maybe she fainted and hit her head. She threw up. . . ."

"Did she have chest pains before she got sick?" the voice asked.

"I don't know. I was asleep. When I woke up, I heard her coughing and getting sick, and when I came into the bathroom, she was passed out on the floor," but as he said the words, he could hear sirens approaching, and all he could do was pray that it was an ambulance for her. "I hear an ambulance . . . is that ours?"

"I hope so. How does she look now? Is she breathing?"

"I'm not sure. . . . She looks so terrible." He was crying, terrified of what was happening, panicked by how she looked. And as he wrestled with everything he felt, the bell rang from downstairs, and he ran to press the buzzer in the hall to let them in. He unlocked the front door, and left it standing wide, and then rushed back to her. When he got back to Anne, nothing had changed, but within instants, the paramedics were on his heels, and standing in the bathroom. There were three of them, from fire rescue, and they pushed him aside and knelt over her. They listened to her heart, checked her eyes, and the man in charge told the other two to get her on the gurney they had brought, and all Robert could hear in the muddle of their words was "defibrillator," as he followed them downstairs. He was still in his pajamas, and he barely had time to grab his coat and put on his shoes, as he shoved his phone into the pocket of his coat, grabbed his wallet off the dresser, and ran after them at a dead run. They already had Anne in the ambulance by the time he came outside, and he just had time to jump in next to her before they pulled away.

"What happened? What's happening to her?" He wondered if she had choked on something she vomited, and had been strangling quietly, but the paramedics told him that she had had a heart attack. And as they explained it to him, one of them tore open her nightgown and put the defibrillator on her chest. Her breasts were exposed, and Robert wanted to cover her, but he knew this was no time to worry about modesty. She looked like she was dying. Her heart had stopped and she was already wearing an oxygen mask as Robert watched in horror as her whole body convulsed, and they did it again. "Oh my God . . . oh my God . . . Anne," he whispered as he stared at her and took her hand in his, "baby . . . please . . . please . . ." Her heart started again then, but it was obvious that she was in dire straits, and Robert had never felt so helpless in his life. Only hours before, they had been having dinner with their friends, and she looked tired, but nothing that would have suggested something as dramatic as this, or he would have taken her to the emergency room right away.

The paramedics were too busy to talk to him, but they seemed satisfied with her condition momentarily, as they spoke to the nearest hospital on their radio, and Robert dialed Eric on his cellular, with shaking hands. It was four-twenty-five in the morning by then, and Eric answered on the second ring.

"I'm in an ambulance, with Anne," Robert said in a shaking voice, "she had a heart attack, and her heart just stopped. They just started it again, oh God, Eric, she's gray and her lips are blue," he was sobbing incoherently, as Eric instantly stood up and turned on the light, and Diana stirred. She was used to the late-night calls he got from the labor room, and she rarely woke up

41

anymore, but something about the tone of his voice was different this time, and she opened an eye, and squinted up at him.

"Is she conscious?" Eric asked quietly.

"No . . . I found her on the bathroom floor . . . I thought maybe she hit her head . . . I don't know . . . Eric, she looks like . . . she . . ." He could barely string the words together.

"Where are they taking her?"

"Lenox Hill, I think."

It was only a few blocks away for him. "I'll be there in five minutes. I'll meet you in the emergency room, or Cardiac ICU. I'll find you . . . and Robert, she'll be okay . . . just hang in." He wanted desperately to reassure him, and hoped he was right.

"Thank you" was all he could say, and he ended the call, as the paramedics held the defibrillator poised again, but her heart kept beating until they arrived at the hospital, and there was already a cardiac team waiting for her on the sidewalk there. They covered her with a blanket, and she was out of the ambulance and into the hospital before Robert could thank anyone, or say anything. The gurney virtually flew past him, and all he could do was run into the hospital behind her. They took her straight up to Coronary ICU, as Robert stood there feeling useless in his overcoat and pajamas. He suddenly looked and felt a thousand years old, and all he wanted to do was be with his beloved Anne. He didn't want to abandon her to strangers.

Within minutes, a resident came to ask him a series of questions, and five minutes later, Eric was standing in the corridor beside him, and Diana was with him. She had woken up the minute she had heard Eric's questions to Robert, and insisted on coming to the hospital with him. They were both wearing jeans and raincoats, and desperately worried faces. But Eric was at least outwardly calm, and knew to ask the right questions. He went inside the coronary unit, and left Robert with Diana. And when he came back, it was obvious that he didn't have good news.

"She's fibrillating again. She's putting up a hell of a battle." It was apparently the second time Anne's heart had stopped since they brought her into the unit. And the resident cardiologist had told Eric he didn't like the look of her vitals. She had been close to gone when they got her. "When did this start?" Eric asked Robert, as Diana held tightly to their friend's hand, and Eric put an arm around him, while Robert cried pitifully as he told them what had happened.

"I don't know. I woke up at four. She was coughing, and I thought she was vomiting by the way she sounded. I waited a few minutes, and then she got very quiet, and when I went in, she was already unconscious."

"Did she have chest pains when you got home last night?" Eric frowned as he asked, not that it mattered now. Whenever it had started, the attack had hit her hard, and there was clearly a doubt in the cardiologist's mind as to whether she would survive. It was not looking good.

"She was just very tired, but she seemed fine otherwise. She talked about the house in the South of France, and going to a movie tomorrow." His mind was spinning, and then he looked down at Diana from his considerable height, but his eyes seemed almost not to see her. He was in shock over everything that had just happened. "I should call the kids, shouldn't I? But I hate to scare them."

"I'll call them," Diana said quietly. "Do you remember their numbers?" He reeled off a series of numbers as Diana jotted them down, and left Robert with Eric when she went to call them. She knew them well enough to assume the responsibility of bearing bad tidings.

"Oh my God," Robert rambled as Eric forced him to sit down, "what if . . ."

"Just wait. People do survive things like this. Try to stay calm. It's not going to help her if you fall apart or get sick. She's going to need you to be strong, Robert."

"I need her," he said in a strangled voice, "I couldn't live without her." Eric was silently praying he wouldn't have to, but that didn't look like a sure thing by any means. He could only imagine how hard this was for him. He knew how devoted they were to each other, and how happy they had been for nearly forty years. Sometimes, like all people who had lived together successfully for that long, they seemed like two halves of the same person.

"You just have to hang on right now," Eric said, standing close to him, and patting his shoulder, as Diana rejoined them. She had reached all three of their children, and they said they would come immediately. Both boys lived on the Upper East Side, and their daughter Amanda lived in SoHo, but at that hour, it would be easy to get cabs, it was five o'clock in the morning by then. It was nearly an hour since Robert had found her, and the nightmare had started.

"Will they let me see her?" Robert said in a voice filled with panic. He had never felt so weak, so unequal to any task. For all intents and purposes, he had always thought of himself as a strong man, as had Anne, but without her, he suddenly felt his whole world, his life, crumbling around him, and all he could think of was how she had looked, lying on the bathroom floor, gray and unconscious.

"They'll let you see her as soon as they can," Eric said reassuringly. "I think they're working pretty hard now, and there's a lot going on. Your being in there will only add to the confusion." Robert nodded, and closed his eyes as Diana sat down on the couch next to him and held his hand tightly. She was praying for Anne, but she didn't want to say as much to Robert. She hadn't even stopped to comb her hair before running out with Eric.

"I want to see her," Robert said finally, with a frantic air, and Eric volunteered to go into the depths of the Coronary ICU and see how Anne was doing. But when he got there, what he saw wasn't a reassuring sight. They had intubated her, and she was on a respirator, and there were half a dozen monitors beeping frantically all around her. They had an IV line in by then, and the full team was working on her, and the head of the team was shouting commands to the others. Eric knew with one glance that there was no way they were going to let Robert in to see her, and for the moment, he thought it was just as well that they didn't. It would have terrified Robert.

When Eric went back out to him again, in the waiting room, both Robert's sons had arrived, with worried faces, and Amanda arrived only a few minutes later. Everyone seemed to have talked to Anne in the past few days, and all of them were stunned. She had seemed fine, healthy, busy as usual, and completely in control, and now, in one instant, she lay fighting for her life, and they were all helpless to save her. Mandy put an arm around her younger brother and cried as they stood in the hallway, and Robert's older son was sitting next to him, as Diana sat on the other side, still holding his hand. But there was nothing any of them could do as they waited.

It was just after seven o'clock when the head cardiologist came to tell them that she had had another massive heart attack, without regaining consciousness, and he didn't need to tell them how grave the situation was, they all knew it. And Robert put his face in his hands and cried. He was completely undone by what had happened, and not ashamed to show it. If loving her would have brought her back, what he felt for her would have done it.

It was a long, grim night, and just after eight o'clock in the morning, as Diana came back from the cafeteria with a tray of coffee for everyone, the cardiologist returned to the waiting room with a solemn expression. Eric saw him first, and knew without a word what had happened, as did Robert.

Robert stood straight up and looked at him, as though wanting to ward off his words before he said them. "No," he said, as though refusing to believe what hadn't even been said yet. "No. I don't want to hear it." He looked terrified, but strong suddenly, and almost angry. His eyes were wild and unfamiliar to all who knew him. It was heartbreaking to see him.

"I'm sorry, Mr. Smith. Your wife didn't survive the second coronary. We did everything we could. She never regained consciousness. We massaged her heart . . . she just gave out on us. I'm so very sorry." Robert stood staring at him, looking as though he were about to collapse, and in an instant Amanda was in his arms, sobbing uncontrollably over the loss of her mother. None of them could believe what had just happened. It seemed impossible, only hours before they had been having dinner with friends, and now she was gone. Robert couldn't even begin to absorb it, and he felt wooden as he held his daughter, and when he looked over her shoulder, all he could see were Eric and Diana, crying, and his two sons with their arms around each other, sobbing.

The doctor told him as gently as possible that he would have to speak to someone about making arrangements, and they would keep Anne there in the meantime. And as Robert listened to him, he began sobbing. "What arrangements?" he asked hoarsely.

"You'll need to call a funeral home, Mr. Smith, and talk to them about it. I'm very sorry," he repeated, and then drifted back to the desk in the ICU to talk to the nurses. There were forms he had to fill out before he went off duty, as Robert and the others stood aimlessly in the waiting room, while other visitors began to drift in. It was nearly nine o'clock on Saturday morning by then, and people were coming to visit other patients.

"Why don't we go back to our place for a while?" Eric suggested quietly, wiping his eyes, and putting a firm arm around Robert. "We can have coffee and talk," he said, eyeing Diana, and she nodded. She took Amanda under her wing, and Robert walked out of the waiting room, flanked by both of his sons, with Eric just behind them. They walked blindly through the hospital, and outside into the winter morning. It was icy cold after the rain the night before, and it looked as though there was another storm brewing. But Robert saw nothing. He felt deaf, dumb, and blind, as he slipped into a cab with his children. Eric and Diana took another just behind them, and five minutes later they were at the Morrisons' apartment.

Diana moved quickly and quietly around her kitchen, making coffee and toast for all of them, as Robert sat in her living room, looking devastated, with the others.

"I just don't understand it," he said as she set a mug of coffee in front of him on the coffee table. "She was fine last night. We had such a good time, and the last thing she said before she went to sleep was how much she was looking forward to the house in France next summer."

"What house in France?" Jeff, his elder son, asked numbly.

"We rented a house in St Tropez with the Donnallys and your parents for next August," Eric explained. "We were looking at pictures of it last night, and your mother seemed fine then. Although now that I think of it, she looked tired and pale, but all New Yorkers do in winter. I didn't think anything of it." Eric was angry at himself now for not suspecting something.

"I asked her on the way home," Robert said, going over it in his mind again, "if she was okay. She seemed exhausted, but she always works so hard, it didn't seem unusual. She was going to sleep late this morning." And now she was sleeping forever. Robert felt a rising sense of panic as he realized that he hadn't asked to see her, but he assumed he would have a chance to later. He hadn't been thinking of anything except the overwhelming loss he had just sustained. And it was as though he felt now that if he played the film back often enough in his head, it would end differently than it just had. As though in viewing it again, he would see that she was more than tired, and be able to save her. But the exercise in torture he had devised was pointless, and they all knew it.

He only took two sips of the coffee, and never touched the toast Diana made them. He couldn't think of eating anything at all, and all he wanted to do now was see her and hold her.

"What do we do now?" Amanda asked, blowing her nose on one of the tissues from the box Diana had discreetly left on the table. Amanda was twenty-five years old, and had never experienced a loss like this one, or any other. Death was entirely unfamiliar to her. Her grandparents had died when she was too small to remember. She hadn't even lost a pet in her entire life. And this was a big one to start with.

"I can take care of some of that for you," Eric said gently. "I'll call Frank Campbell this morning." It was a prestigious funeral parlor that had taken care of New Yorkers for years, even some as illustrious as Judy Garland. "Do you have any idea what you want to do, Robert? Do you want her cremated?" The question demolished him in an instant. He didn't want her cremated, he wanted her alive again, in the Morrisons' living room, asking them all why they were being so silly. But this wasn't silly. It was unbearable, unthinkable, intolerable, to her husband, and her children. They were actually handling it better than he was.

"Can I do something to help, Dad?" Jeff offered quietly, and his younger brother Mike tried to rise to the occasion. They had both called their wives, and told them the news, and a few minutes later, Diana slipped away to call Pascale and John. They were stunned when she told them that Anne had died that morning. At first, they couldn't understand it.

"Anne? But she was fine last night," Pascale insisted, just as everyone else had. "I can't believe it. . . . What happened?" Diana told her as much as she knew, and Pascale was crying when she went to tell John, while he was reading the paper. Half an hour later, they arrived at the Morrisons' too, and it was after one o'clock when Robert finally went back to his apartment to get dressed. And when he saw the lights on, and the towels on the floor in the bathroom, which he had put there to cover and warm her, he broke into agonized sobs again, and when he lay on their bed, he could smell her perfume on his pillow. It was all beyond bearing.

Eric went to Campbell's with him that afternoon, and helped him go through the unbearable agonies that were

51

required of him, making decisions, ordering flowers, picking a casket. He chose a handsome mahogany, with a white velvet interior. The whole thing was a nightmare, and they told him that he could see his wife later that afternoon when she arrived from the hospital. And when he did, with Diana standing next to him, it completely unglued him. He held Anne's lifeless form to him, while Diana watched them, silently crying. That night he went to Jeff's to have dinner with his children. Jeff and his wife insisted that he spend the night with them, and he was relieved to do it. Mandy was staying with Mike and his wife Susan at their apartment. None of them wanted to be alone, and they were grateful to have each other.

The Donnallys and Morrisons had dinner together that night, still unable to believe what had happened. Only the night before Anne had been with them, and now she was gone, and Robert was a shambles.

"I hate to bring up something so tactless under the circumstances," Diana said cautiously as they looked mournfully at their plates and scarcely touched the Chinese takeout they'd ordered. No one was hungry, and at Jeff's house, Robert was literally starving. He hadn't touched food since the night before and didn't want to. "But I was just thinking about what we should do with the house in St Tropez."

"As long as you're being tactless," John looked as grim

as the others, "I will be too. The house is too expensive divided by two and not three couples. We'll have to let it go," he said firmly, as Pascale glanced uncomfortably at her husband.

"I don't think we can do that now," she said in a whisper.

"Why not? We haven't even told them yet we'd take it." They had agreed to send a fax from Anne's office on Monday.

"Yes, we did," Pascale said, looking sheepish.

"What does that mean?" John looked at her blankly.

"It's such a great house, and I was afraid someone else would take it, so I asked my mother to put a deposit on it as soon as the agent called me. I was sure we'd all love it."

"Terrific," John said through clenched teeth. "Your mother hasn't paid for a tube of toothpaste in years, without having you either send it or pay for it, and suddenly she's putting deposits on houses? *Before* we even agree to it?" He looked at Pascale sternly, unable to believe what she was saying.

"I told her we'd pay her back," Pascale said softly, looking apologetically at her husband. But the house had turned out to be every bit as good as the agent promised, and they had loved the pictures of it, so she hadn't been mistaken.

"Just tell her to get her money back," John said firmly.

"I can't. It's not refundable, they explained that before I had her pay it."

"Oh for chrissake, Pascale, why the hell did you do that?" He was furious with her, but, he was obviously far more upset over Anne's death, and didn't know how to express it. "Well, you can just damn well pay for it yourself, out of your own money. No one is going to want to go there now, and Robert certainly won't without Anne. It's over. Forget the house."

"Maybe not," Diana said quietly. "It's six and a half months from now. Robert may be feeling a lot better by then, and it might do him good to get away, to someplace he's never been before, with all of us to keep him company and comfort him. I think we should do it." Eric looked pensively at her, and nodded.

"I think you're right," he seconded her opinion, but John didn't.

"And if he doesn't want to go? Then we get stuck with two very expensive shares. I'm not going. And I'm not paying." John glowered.

"Then I will," Pascale glared at him as she said it. "You're just so cheap, John Donnally, you are using this as an excuse not to spend money. I'll pay our share, and you can stay home, or visit your mother in Boston."

"Since when did you get so grand?" he said in a tone that upset her profoundly. But like the others, she was upset about Anne, and not her husband.

"I think we need to be together, and Robert will need us more than ever," Pascale insisted, and both Morrisons agreed with her, and tried to get John to go along with it, but he was too stubborn.

"I'm not going," he insisted.

"Then don't. The four of us will," Pascale said calmly, smiling sadly at Eric and Diana. "We'll send you postcards from the Riviera."

"Take your mother."

"Maybe I will," Pascale said, and then turned to the others. "It's agreed then. We'll go to St Tropez in August." It was the least of their problems for the moment, but it was comforting somehow to think of something more pleasant. All they could think about other than that was the loss of their beloved friend, and Robert. There wasn't much they could do for him, but they could offer him their support. And although it felt like something of a betrayal to go to St Tropez without Anne, Pascale said she had the feeling that Anne would have wanted them to do it, and take Robert.

"We may have a tough time convincing him to go with us," Diana suggested reasonably, "but we've got plenty of time to talk about it. Let's just go ahead and rent it, and discuss it with him later." And by then, she suspected, John would have relented too. But it was so sad to think of the five of them going, and not Anne. It was inconceivable to think that she would no longer be with them.

55

The Donnallys went home shortly after that, and they called Robert at Jeff's and told him that they were thinking of him. But he was too upset to talk to them for very long, and Pascale could hear that he'd been crying. All day in fact, and she wished there was something she could do for him, but there wasn't. She promised to meet him at the funeral home the next day for the "viewing." The funeral had been set for Tuesday. Robert had had Jeff call Anne's partners in the law firm, and his daughters-in-law had called long lists of people to tell them, before the obituary came out the next day, on Sunday. Robert had written it himself, and Mike had dropped it off at *The New York Times* that afternoon.

It was incomprehensible, Robert thought to himself, as he got into the bed in Jeff and Elizabeth's guest room. He felt completely disoriented from grief, and crying, and lack of food, and as he lay there thinking about her, he had never in his entire life felt so devastated or so lonely. Thirty-eight wonderful years had ended in a single instant. And Robert was absolutely sure, without a specter of a doubt, that his life was over too.

3

ANNE'S FUNERAL WAS HELD at St James Church on Madison Avenue on Tuesday afternoon. Robert sat in the front pew with his children, his daughters-in-law, and all five of his grandchildren were there, as were his four best friends. The church was filled with people who knew both of them, people Anne had worked with, clients, class-mates, and old friends. And Robert looked grief-stricken as he entered, with his daughter on his arm. They were both crying, as were his sons. And in the silence of the church, the people closest to them could hear Pascale sob. John sat stoically next to her, with silent tears coursing down his cheeks.

The Morrisons sat next to them in the second pew, with damp eyes, silently holding hands. It was inconceivable to all of them that Anne was gone. The sacred circle of their friendship had been disrupted, an important piece was missing now. They had all lost a cherished friend.

Danielle Steel

The service was brief and touching, and when they emerged from the church to follow the casket to the hearse, it was snowing outside. It had already been a hard winter, but this particular day seemed exceptionally bleak. Robert went to the cemetery with his children, and left Anne there, after a few brief words from the minister, who had known them since they were married. And then Robert said his last good-byes. He looked like a zombie as he finally walked, with blind eyes, toward the car.

And after the cemetery, all of them went to the Morrisons', to have lunch with the people the Morrisons had invited to be with them. Robert looked as though he was on autopilot as he moved through the crowd, and before anyone left, he disappeared. He didn't even tell his children when he left. John Donnally took him home, and hated to leave him there, so he stayed.

Robert sat down heavily on the couch and stared into space. He was too bereft at that moment in time to even cry. He just sat, with unseeing eyes.

"Can I get you anything?" John asked quietly, wishing Pascale were there. She was so much better at this kind of thing. But he had sensed correctly that Robert hadn't wanted anyone else there, probably not even John.

"No, thanks." John wasn't sure if he should stay for a while, and just sit with him, or leave. And Robert said nothing at all. Not knowing what else to do, John got

58

him a glass of water and set it in front of him, which Robert appeared not to see. And then finally, he leaned his head back against the couch and closed his eyes. He spoke in the silence of the room, with his eyes closed, feeling the full agony of his words. "I always thought I'd die first. She was younger, and she always seemed so strong. It never occurred to me that I'd lose her." People had been telling him for four days that he would never lose her, that her spirit would live on, but in fact it was all too clear that he had. And then he looked at John with immeasurable pain. "John, what am I going to do now?" He had no idea how to live without her. After thirty-eight years, she was an integral part of him, like his soul.

"I think you get through it day by day," John said, sitting down next to him on the couch, "that's all you can do. And one day, you feel better. Maybe it's never the same, but you go on. You have your kids, your friends. People survive it." He didn't want to tell him that he might even remarry one day, though in Robert's case that seemed unlikely. He had loved her for too long, and he wasn't that kind of man. But even without someone else in his life one day, he had to go on. He had no choice. All John could do was pray that it didn't kill him, that he didn't just give up on his own life.

"Maybe I should retire. I can't imagine going back to

work." He couldn't imagine doing anything without her now. His most important reason for living was gone.

"It's too soon to make that decision," John said wisely. "Don't do anything yet." If nothing else, he needed the distraction of his work, or he himself might die. John had seen that happen to others before, and he was seriously worried about his friend.

"I should sell the apartment. How can I live here without her?" His eyes were open and filled with tears again.

"You can stay with us for a while if you like, till you figure out what you want to do." But in truth, Robert wanted to be here with his memories of her. Pascale and Diana had already offered to help Amanda go through her mother's clothes, but even that seemed too much to face, and Robert had said he didn't want anything disturbed. It was a comfort to him to see her things in the closet, her dressing gown on the hook in the bathroom, her toothbrush in the cup. It allowed him to delude himself that she was just away somewhere, at a conference maybe, and coming back. But the brutal fact they all knew he had to face at some point was that she was gone for good.

John sat with him for a long time, and they said nothing, and then finally as the room grew dark, Robert drifted off to sleep on the couch. John didn't want to leave him, and he sat quietly in Robert's study, glancing through some of his books. And at six o'clock he called Pascale.

"How is he?" As they all were, she was desperately worried.

"He's asleep, he's emotionally exhausted. I didn't want to leave him. What do you think I should do?" He relied on Pascale's judgment in matters of the heart.

"Stay there with him. I think you should spend the night." John had already considered the same thing. "Don't wake him up. Do you want me to bring food?"

"There must be something here," he said vaguely, but he wasn't sure and hadn't looked.

"I'll bring some sandwiches over, and some soup," she said firmly, and for once he didn't make any cracks about her cooking, he was grateful to her. Losing Anne had reminded all of them how precious life and their partners were. He felt a little out of his depth in terms of how best to help Robert. They all did. "I'll see you in a while."

And when Pascale arrived carrying a shopping bag and a baguette under her arm, Robert had just woken up. He looked disoriented and exhausted, but the long nap had done him good. He hadn't slept properly since Friday night. But when he saw the soup and sandwiches Pascale had set out for them in the kitchen, he said he couldn't eat. She could see easily that he had already lost weight, and seemed too thin.

"You have to. Your children need you, Robert. And so do we. You can't get sick."

"Why not?" he asked grimly. "What difference does it make?"

"A lot. To us. Now be good, and have some soup." She spoke to him as though he were a child, and he sat down at the kitchen table, and began eating the soup. He only got halfway through it, and refused the sandwiches she'd made, but at least he'd had some nourishment. And then she suggested that John spend the night with him.

"He doesn't have to do that. You two should go home. I'm fine." It was not a word anyone would have used to describe him, but it was a noble thought.

"John wants to stay here," she urged, but Robert was insistent, and the Donnallys finally left at ten o'clock. They both looked drained in the cab on the way home. "I'm so worried about him," Pascale said. "What if he just gives up and dies? People do that sometimes."

"He won't," John answered, trying to believe what he said. "He can't. He'll get over it eventually, not completely maybe, but enough to function reasonably well. Maybe that's all we can expect." It seemed a sad statement on Robert's future life.

"I'm not so sure," Pascale said, wiping tears off her cheeks again. It was all so sad. Who could have known that tragedy would strike them, that Anne would leave them, without warning, and so soon? It made Pascale snuggle closer to her husband, as the cab drove them home. It was a brutal reminder of how ephemeral life was, how quickly interrupted, how fragile, of their own mortality. And the message had not gone unheard.

Pascale and John, Eric and Diana, each called him every day. But none of them saw him for the next three weeks. He couldn't bear being alone in the apartment and slept at Jeff's for the first few weeks. He kept to a schedule centered around his children, and stayed home from work—he didn't go back to the bench for a month. And when he did, finally, he saw the Donnallys and Morrisons again. He had just moved back into his apartment that week. And Anne had been gone for a month.

They were all shocked when they saw him, he had lost a lot of weight, and his eyes looked ravaged. All Pascale could do when she saw him was hold him tightly and fight back her own tears. His grief was a raw reminder of the loss of their friend. And their hearts went out to him.

"So, what have you all been up to?" Robert tried to sound interested, but his eyes said he didn't care. It was hard to relate to their doings, to think of their lives with each other, without feeling the knife stab of pain over the enormity of his loss. But in spite of that, he was happy to see them again. They brought him comfort, and by the end of the evening, he was even smiling at some of John's tasteless jokes, and renewed complaints about Pascale. But they all seemed mellower, gentler, and more loving to each other, and to him, than they had before. The message of Anne's death had been loud and clear to all of them.

"I got more pictures of the house in St Tropez yesterday," Pascale said casually over coffee, testing the waters, although she knew it was still too soon, and their rental was still five and a half months away, a long distance still to travel on Robert's map of grief.

She chatted on for a few minutes about the house, and then Robert looked at her quietly with eyes filled with sorrow. "I'm not going with you" was all he said. It would have reminded him too much of the summer he wanted so much to spend with Anne in France, and had once before.

"You don't need to make that decision yet," Diana said softly, glancing at Eric, as he nodded, and joined in.

"If you don't come, John will make life miserable for the rest of us. He's too cheap to pay for the house split two ways. You may have to come, for our sakes," Eric said with a grin, and Robert managed a small, wintry smile.

"Maybe Diana can organize a fund-raiser to pay for the rent," he suggested.

"Now there's an idea," John said, brightening at the suggestion, and all five of them laughed. "Maybe your mother could stand on the corner with a cup filled with pencils, and give us a hand," he said to Pascale as her eyes flashed. But it was a hint at least of the banter and the laughter that had come before, and hadn't been heard now in a month.

"Actually, I'd be willing to honor our commitment, and pay our part. Anne was the one who convinced the rest of you. I don't mind paying our share. I just don't want to go," Robert said.

"Don't be silly, Robert," Diana said clearly, as Pascale flashed a look at her.

"Actually, I think that would be very nice," Pascale spoke up, as the others stared at her. "I'm sure Anne would have wanted you to do that too." Robert nodded, numbly. In his scrambled state, it sounded reasonable to him. Why should they suffer financially because of her death?

"Tell me how much it is, and I'll send you a check," he said simply, and the subject of conversation moved on to something else. But even John looked uncomfortable about it when he mentioned it to Pascale after the others left.

"Don't you think that's a little crude, asking Robert to pay for a house he isn't going to use? You say I'm cheap, that little trick seemed awfully French." His eyes told her that he disapproved of what she'd done, but she looked unembarrassed, as she cleared the glasses they had left.

"If he pays, he'll come, even if he doesn't think so now." And with that, John smiled at her. She was a very clever girl.

"Do you really think so?"

"Wouldn't you?"

"Me?" John laughed at himself. "Hell, if I paid, I'd want to get my money's worth. But Robert is a little nobler than I am. I don't think he'll come."

"I do. He doesn't know it yet, but he will. And it will do him a lot of good." She sounded sure.

"If he does, I hope he doesn't bring all his kids, now that she's gone. His grandchildren are so damn noisy, and Susan gets on my nerves." She got on Pascale's nerves too, and so did his other daughter-in-law, sometimes even Amanda and the grandchildren were loud, but right now, Pascale didn't care.

"It doesn't matter. Let's just hope he'll be there."

"You know, I'm glad you did that," John said, looking tenderly at her. "When you said it to him, I almost choked on my coffee. I thought maybe you've been living with me for too long," he admitted with a grin.

"Not long enough," she said softly, and leaned toward him to give him a kiss. Ever since Anne had died, she was reminded of how much he meant to her, and John had been thinking much the same thing. Despite their frequent differences, they were very lucky, and knew it. Life was short, they had all been reminded, and sometimes very sweet.

4

THE GROUP SAW Robert for dinner weekly for the next three months, and called him daily for the first two. He was better than he had been, though sad certainly, and he talked about Anne whenever they saw him. But the stories had gone from mournful to funny, and although he still cried sometimes when he talked about her, he was able to smile now too.

And he was very busy at work. He was still talking about selling the apartment, but he had not yet put away her things. When Pascale and John picked him up for dinner there one night, she saw Anne's nightgown in the bathroom, her hairbrush on the dresser, and the hall closet was still full of her coats and boots. But at least he was keeping busy, seeing his children, and he seemed more animated now with his friends.

They were beginning to talk about the summer, and

urging him to join them in St Tropez, but he said he had too much work. But just as he had promised, he had sent them his check, to pay for his share of the house in St Tropez. Robert said he was going to stay in New York that summer instead. It had been four months since Anne's death. He had been busy with her estate, and had set up a charitable foundation in her name, to give money for the causes that meant so much to her, mostly battered women and kids. And he was animated when he spoke of it to them.

"New York in the summer is pretty rough," Eric said amiably, although he admitted that he might have to cut the trip short as well. He said he had been unusually busy in the office, and one of his partners had been sick for several months. Diana was unhappy about it, but had decided that if Eric left early, she would stay on in France with John and Pascale.

"It's going to be pretty sad with just three of us there if Eric has to leave," Diana said, looking worried. She had seemed unusually stressed to Pascale for the past month, but she knew Diana was planning a huge event for Sloan-Kettering, and working on it nights and weekends. "Robert, I really think you ought to come. Anne would have wanted you to, and you can bring the kids."

"We'll see" was all he said. It was the first hopeful sign they'd heard.

"Do you think he will?" they asked each other after he left. He said he had to get to bed early, he had a long day ahead the next day, in court. And he had told them with some amusement that Amanda had asked him to escort her to a black-tie charity event, the premiere of a major film. She and her most recent boyfriend had just broken up, and she didn't have a date. The others had teased him about being glamorous and going to movie premieres, and he said he wasn't looking forward to the party, but he had heard that it was a terrific film.

And he mentioned it when they met again the following week.

"So how was the premiere?" Eric asked him. Eric was looking particularly well, relaxed and happy, despite his long work hours, and sleepless nights covering for his partner, though Diana looked tired and had lost weight. She seemed quieter than usual. And Pascale was concerned, although she didn't mention it to her. They all seemed to worry more about each other now since Anne's death. But they all noticed that Robert was looking better than he had in a long time.

"It was interesting," he admitted. "There must have been five hundred people there, and the party afterward was a zoo. But I think Mandy had a good time. She met some of the actors, I think she knows one of the producers, and some very good-looking guy in a tuxedo without a tie asked her for a date. I think my services as escort will be dispensed with shortly." But in the meantime, he was taking her to another event, and Pascale couldn't help wondering if Mandy was being clever about keeping her father entertained. In spite of the fact that he was still obviously sad over Anne, it kept him distracted and amused. And it gave Pascale an idea.

She called Amanda the next morning, and suggested that she come to St Tropez with her father. "It will do him a lot of good."

"It might," she said pensively. "I think he's doing better, but he says he can't sleep." Amanda was worried about him, and Pascale had correctly guessed that Mandy was doing everything she could to keep him occupied. "He actually did pretty well at the premiere we went to last week. He won't admit it, but I think he had fun. I lost track of him after a while. He circulated pretty well on his own."

"Well, see what you can do about St Tropez," Pascale suggested. "I think that would do him good too."

"Yeah," Mandy laughed, "and me too. Dad said the house comes with a boat. He said the pictures were gorgeous. It sounds like a great trip. I'd love to come."

"We have lots of room for you, and we'd love it," Pascale said warmly, and Amanda said she would see what she could do.

But the following week when they were scheduled to

have dinner with Robert, he canceled, and said he had too much work to do. In the end, it was just as well, as Eric had to deliver three babies that night and would have had to miss dinner, and Pascale came down with the flu.

She was still feeling woozy when Diana called her, and said she had something to tell Pascale that would knock her off her feet.

"You're pregnant!" Pascale said with a tone of envy, and Diana laughed.

"I sure hope not. If I am, the hormones I've been taking work better than I think." She had gone through change of life two years before. For Diana, pregnancy was no longer an option, and it never had been for Pascale. "No, but it's almost as amazing as that. I had dinner with Samantha last night, after you all canceled and Eric had to work. We went to the Mezza Luna, or at least we were going to. We sneaked off somewhere else after we got there, but who do you think was there?"

"I don't know. . . . Tom Cruise, and he asked you for a date."

"Damn close. Robert. He was having dinner with a woman. And he was laughing and smiling. I didn't recognize the woman, but Sam did. You're not going to believe this. It was Gwen Thomas."

"The actress?" Pascale sounded as though she'd been hit by a bomb, and she had. "Are you sure?"

"No. But it looked like her. Sam was sure that was who it was." She was beautiful, and young, and had looked deeply engrossed in conversation with him. And he looked very happy with her.

"How do you suppose he knows her?" He had never mentioned her before. Nor had he mentioned having dinner with women in the months since Anne's death. Pascale couldn't help wondering if this was a first for him. It had to be.

"Isn't she the star of the movie he saw with Mandy last week?" Diana inquired.

"I think so," Pascale said, sinking back onto her pillows again, staring pensively into space. "God, how stupid if he starts going out with actresses and starlets and models. He's so vulnerable, and so naïve in a way. He and Anne were married forever. He knows nothing about that world. Anne always said he had hardly dated before they met. He certainly knows nothing about the dating scene." Nor did any of them. They had all been married for so many years.

"No, he doesn't," Diana agreed with her completely, and vowed silently to protect him, for Anne's sake, and his own. She'd have expected it of them. He seemed the last person in the world to be going out with a famous actress or anyone at this point. It seemed impossible to imagine him with anyone but Anne.

"How old is she?" Pascale sounded genuinely worried, fearing that Diana would say she was twenty-two, but she knew she was older than that. She was a very beautiful woman, and had recently been enjoying a huge success. She had won an Oscar the previous year.

"I think she's in her late thirties, maybe forty. She doesn't look it though. She looks Sam's age."

"How stupid of him. He's way out of his league, if he starts going out with women like that. Did they look amorous?"

"No," Diana said fairly, "they didn't. They looked like friends," she said, sounding slightly relieved.

"I wonder how he met her."

"Maybe at the premiere."

The two women talked for the better part of an hour, about the dangers and the pitfalls and the traps that would be set for their friend, and they vowed to give him a lecture when the opportunity presented itself. It seemed more important than ever now to get him to St Tropez.

"I wonder if Mandy knows he went out with her, or even that he met her," Diana pondered.

"She said she lost track of him at the premiere," Pascale volunteered. "I'll invite him for dinner next week, and see if he says anything about her. Maybe we should ask him. Did he see you?"

"No," Diana admitted, "I was so shocked, we literally ran away. I didn't want to intrude. And in a way, I guess it's a good thing he's getting out and seeing women. But I just don't want him to get hurt." Imagining him in the clutches of a movie star terrified them both.

"Absolutely," Pascale agreed. "There are lots of nice women we all know and can introduce him to, if he's ready. I just didn't think he was." It had come as a huge surprise to both of them.

And Pascale was relieved when he agreed to meet them for dinner the next week. He sounded normal, and as solemn as ever, when she called him in his office at the court.

Much to everyone's surprise, when they had dinner, he mentioned meeting Gwen.

"Who is she?" John looked blank when Robert said it, and both women were carefully studying his face to see if it meant anything to him.

"She won an Oscar," Pascale said to her husband, with a look of contempt. "Everyone knows who she is. She's very pretty," and then she turned to Robert. "How did you meet her?"

"With Mandy at a film premiere," Robert said innocently as Pascale and Diana's eyes met. It was exactly what they'd thought. "She's an interesting woman. She lived in England for a long time, and did Shakespeare. And then she worked on Broadway before she got into movies. She's very levelheaded, and well read." Diana looked worried as she listened, and Pascale's eyes narrowed with suspicion instantly.

"You know a lot about her," she said casually, as John shot her a look.

"What does she look like?" John asked with growing interest, wondering exactly what she meant to him, or if they'd gone to bed.

"She's attractive," Robert said without any particular passion. "She has red hair. She's divorced." Pascale gulped.

"How old is she?" Diana asked calmly.

"Forty-one," he said, eating his dinner. Their guesses had been correct. "She's been living in California, and she just moved back to New York. She seems kind of lonely. She doesn't know anyone here." Pascale and Diana were certain that was just a ploy to reel him in.

"Are you going to see her again?" Pascale couldn't resist asking, with a look of innocence.

"I don't know," he said vaguely, "she's busy. So am I. She's starting another movie in September, and she's going to travel this summer with friends. I think Anne would have liked her," he said calmly, smiling at his friends. He hadn't an inkling of the turmoil in the two women's minds. They concealed it well, from him at least.

"Robert," Diana said cautiously, not sure where to start, "you have to be careful. There are a lot of very manipulative, very artful women out there. You haven't been out in the big bad dating world in a long time." She adopted a sisterly tone for her brief speech, and he smiled.

"And I'm not 'dating' now," he said, looking her in the eye. "She's just a friend." What he said ended the conversation, and after they went their separate ways after dinner, Eric told Diana that she'd been out of line.

"He's a big boy. He has a right to do what he wants. And if he can snag some movie star for his first date, more power to him." Eric looked both admiring and amused.

"He doesn't know what he's doing," Diana insisted. "God only knows what kind of barracuda that girl is. He didn't even mention if she had kids."

"What difference does that make?"

"Because it would mean she's stable, and at least a halfway decent person."

"Pascale doesn't have kids, and she's a great person. That's a silly thing to say. Lots of 'decent' women don't have kids."

"In Pascale's case, that's different, and you know it. I'm just worried about him."

"So am I. But if he's going out with women, it's a terrific

sign, and I feel a lot better. Why don't you and Pascale mind your own business and leave the poor guy alone?"

"We wanted to warn him for his own good," she insisted.

"This is the best thing that could happen to him. And maybe she's a nice girl." He preferred to assume the best rather than the worst, unlike Diana and Pascale who already hated her, in defense of Anne.

"A movie star? Are you kidding? How likely is that?" Diana persisted in her point of view.

"Not very likely, I'll admit. But at least he'll have some fun with her." There was a twinkle in his eye as he said it, and as she went to her bathroom to undress, Diana looked annoyed. The fraternity of men always stuck together, and as long as Robert could have some "fun," who cared what kind of tramp Gwen Thomas was? Clearly, Eric didn't, and John was saying much the same thing to Pascale at their home.

"Oh, *alors!*" Pascale was arguing with him. "And what if she is going to break his heart, or use him?"

"Use him for what?" John said in obvious irritation. "Hell, I can think of worse fates than being 'used' by a movie star."

"Well, I can't. Robert is a kind, loving, decent, honorable man, and an innocent."

"Maybe she is too."

"Mon oeil." My eye. "You must be drunk. Or maybe you're jealous of him."

"Oh for chrissake. The poor guy has been heartbroken over Anne. Let him have some fun."

"Not," Pascale looked daggers at him, "with the wrong girl."

"Give the poor guy a break. He'll probably never even see her again. I'm sure a sixty-three-year-old superior court judge isn't her idea of a hot ticket to romance. Maybe he was telling the truth, and they're just friends."

"We have to get him out of New York, and make him come to St Tropez," she said firmly.

And with that, John laughed at her, and couldn't resist teasing her. "Maybe he'll bring her."

"Over my dead body, and Diana's," she said nobly, and John shook his head as he got into bed.

"God help him. The vice squad is here to protect him, poor bastard. I hope for his sake that he doesn't come to St Tropez."

"You have to convince him to come," Pascale looked imploringly at her husband. "We owe that much to Anne, to protect him from this girl." Like Diana, she had become a zealot overnight, hell-bent on protecting their friend.

"Don't worry, there will be others. At least I hope so for his sake. What would you like me to do, get you a voodoo doll so you can protect him? I'm sure I can find one somewhere."

"Then get it," Pascale said, looking righteous and enraged. "We have to do everything we can." She was now on a sacred mission, and as he put an arm around her in their big cozy bed, all John could do was laugh at her.

5

THE LAST DINNER the Morrisons and Donnallys shared with Robert was at the Four Seasons, just before Pascale left in June. They talked about a variety of subjects, and inevitably, they brought up the house in St Tropez. Robert still insisted he didn't want to go there, and John reminded him that he'd paid a third of it, so he might as well come.

"That was just to cover Anne's obligations," he said, looking sad again. "She wanted so much to go. She would have loved it." He had a faraway look as he spoke to them.

"So would you," John said matter-of-factly. "I didn't want to go either. I told Pascale I wouldn't go when I found out she'd put a deposit on it before I'd agreed to it. But what the hell," he looked a little sheepish as he said it. He had long since reimbursed her mother and agreed to go. "It'll be fun. Why don't you come with us? I don't think Anne would have wanted you not to go." She had been far more generous of spirit than that, as they all knew.

"Maybe," Robert said quietly, thinking about it. "It might be fun for Amanda. Maybe she'd join me for part of it at least. I don't have to stay the whole time."

"There's enough room for Jeff and Mike to come too, if they come in shifts. We have plenty of room. I think Katherine and her husband will join us for a few days too." As Diana said it, Pascale and John exchanged a look. She knew John wasn't in love with the idea of entertaining their kids. But after a quelling glance from Pascale, he didn't say a thing.

"The boys go to Shelter Island in the summer, and they wouldn't have time to come to France. But Mandy would. I'll ask her. Maybe if she comes with me, it would do me good."

"It would do you good either way," Diana said. Pascale had noticed again that night that she was looking strained. But Eric seemed in good spirits, and he was being very sweet to her. But Pascale noticed that Diana was cool to him, which was unlike her. Normally, they were both affectionate and warm.

"I'll let you know in a few days" was all Robert would say. And he called Pascale the day before she left in June, and told her that Mandy had agreed. She was going to be with them for five days. And he wasn't sure yet, but he thought he might stay for two weeks.

"You can stay as long as you want." Pascale was delighted. "It's your house too."

"We'll see." And then he surprised her with what he said next. "I might bring a friend." There was a long pause after he said it, as Pascale struggled to find the right words to ask him what he meant.

"A friend?"

"I don't know yet. I'll let you know when I'm sure." Pascale wanted to ask him who it was, but somehow didn't dare. And she couldn't help but wonder if it was a woman or a man. She knew it couldn't be Gwen Thomas because he had just met her. But she wondered now if he was seeing someone else. She knew he was still grieving for Anne, and he looked devastated when he talked about her, but at the last dinner she had noticed that he seemed to be doing very well. He was getting out more than he had in years, seeing people, going to dinners, playing tennis. He looked younger and healthier than he had before, and being thinner actually suited him very well. It was very odd now to think of him as a single man, and she had to admit he was very attractive, and he suddenly seemed more youthful than he had when he was with Anne.

Pascale gave him her number in Paris and told him that she was going to St Tropez two days before their lease began. The owners had said she could get there early, to open the house and settle in. They hadn't used it for the past two years.

"I'll have everything ready by the time you get there." John and the Morrisons were arriving on the first of August, and Robert said he was planning to fly over on the third. And Mandy would probably arrive with him for her five days.

"Call me if you need anything," he said, and then had to rush back into court before she could inquire again about his "friend." She didn't even know when they might come, or for how long, if at all.

And a few minutes later, she called Diana to tell her he was coming, and Diana said she was thrilled. But Pascale thought she sounded distracted and tense, and finally Pascale decided to ask her what she'd been wondering for a while. "Is anything wrong?"

Diana hesitated only for a fraction of a second and then insisted that everything was fine. And after that, Pascale told her about Robert's "friend."

"What kind of friend?" Diana sounded puzzled by what Pascale said.

"I don't know. I didn't have the courage to ask him. Maybe it's just another judge, or a lawyer. It's probably a man."

"I hope it's not that actress," Diana said, sounding worried, but she agreed with Pascale that it couldn't be. They hardly knew each other, and it was much too soon for him to be taking her anywhere, let alone to France. By the time they all got to St Tropez, Anne would have been gone for less than seven months.

"I'm glad Mandy is coming with him, that'll be good for him." Although possibly less good for them. She was a sweet girl, and loved her father, but she'd had some conflict with her mother over the years, and sometimes it extended to her mother's friends as well. And having a girl her age around wasn't always easy for them.

"He doesn't really need Mandy," Pascale said practically, "he has us. And she's a little difficult sometimes. She used to get on Anne's nerves too." Anne had had some very tough years with her. The boys had always been easier for her.

"That's all right, she was younger then, and it'll only be for five days, it'll make him happy. I'm just glad he decided to come," Diana said generously.

"Me too," Pascale said, sounding pleased. It had taken five months to convince him, after the death of his wife. And in another six weeks, they'd all be in France together, much to Pascale's delight.

"Call me when you see the house," Diana insisted, and Pascale promised to do that. "I'll bet it's terrific," she said, sounding excited, and Pascale laughed. She was still concerned about Diana, but she just hoped it wasn't a problem with her health. After Anne's death, she was more anxious than usual about her friend. She assumed that whatever had been bothering her lately, they would talk about in France.

"If it isn't terrific, John will kill me. He's still crying over what we spent," Pascale added with a laugh.

"It's worth every penny of it. He just does that so we know it's him." The others had paid their shares without complaint, and thought it a fair price, but not John. He was still fuming over what it cost when Pascale left for France.

As always, she reveled in being home again, seeing her old friends, going to her favorite restaurants and shops. She spent an afternoon in the Louvre, looking at new exhibits, and dug around in some antique shops on the Left Bank. She went to the theater, and enjoyed a number of quiet evenings with her mother, grandmother, and aunt. Her visits to Paris recharged her batteries for the whole year. And for once, she found her mother in fairly decent health. And not unlike what John said about his mother-in-law, Pascale's mother complained endlessly about him. According to Pascale's mother, he was too short, too fat, didn't work hard enough, didn't make enough money, dressed like an American, and had never made the effort to learn French. Pascale was used to defending them to each other, and turned a deaf ear while her mother made mincemeat of him. And she didn't say anything to John about it when she called him, but he managed to hurl a few insults at his mother-in-law while he had Pascale on the phone. They were a perfect pair. And through it all, Pascale's aunt said nothing. She was stone deaf, so she couldn't hear what her sister said about him, and she had always thought John a perfectly pleasant man. She was only sorry for them that they had never had children, but Pascale didn't seem to mind. And Pascale's grandmother slept most of the time and had always thought John was very nice.

Whenever she was at home with her family, Pascale seemed to become even more French. Her English got a little rough around the edges, and she forgot familiar words when she talked to John. Her accent got thicker, and she stocked up on French novels and read them late into the night. She ate all her favorite meals, and smoked Gauloises. Every movement, every gesture, every expression, every word, became unmistakably French.

And by the time she left for the South of France at the end of July, she was relaxed and in great form. She had lost a few pounds, in spite of the big dinners she ate, and the cheese and desserts she loved, but she got so much exercise walking all over Paris that she looked better than ever. And the day before Pascale left for St Tropez, her aunt and mother left for Italy, as they always did. Pascale quietly left the apartment, her grandmother was asleep, as usual, and she told the nurse where she could be reached in the South of France.

The flight to Nice was filled to the gills, with couples and families and children, mountains of luggage, and endless shopping bags with straw hats and food, and everything imaginable. Every seat was taken, but people seemed in good spirits. Like most French people, almost all of them had a month's vacation and were heading south for the month. And as many as possible had brought their dogs along. No one except the English loved their dogs more than the French. The only difference was that the English treated their dogs like dogs. The French took them to restaurants, fed them at the table, carried them in handbags, and fluffed their hair. The dogs on the plane proceeded to bark at each other and drive everyone else on the flight insane. But Pascale didn't seem to mind it, she sat looking out the window, thinking about how much fun they were going to have in St Tropez. As a child, she had summered in St Jean Cap-Ferrat and Antibes. St Tropez had always been racier, and a little farther away. It was going to be at least a two-hour drive from Nice. And in traffic, it would be considerably worse. The easiest way to get there from the rest of the Riviera was by boat.

When they landed at the Nice airport, Pascale collected her bags. She had bought some new beach clothes in Paris, which added a third suitcase to the two she had brought from the States. And she was hoping to find a porter to help her get to the car rental and then to her car.

She knew that if John had been with her, he would have made her carry at least two of her bags, and complained while he juggled the rest. She was carrying a large Hermès tote, and another big straw beach bag. It was undeniably a lot of stuff. And the porter happily put it in the trunk and on the backseat of her rented Peugeot. And half an hour after she had landed, Pascale was on her way to St Tropez.

Predictably at that time of year, the roads were crowded, there were lots of convertibles, handsome men, and pretty women, and a veritable herd of Deux Chevaux, the tiny little cars that seemed to multiply like rabbits in France. But John thought they weren't safe. Although he complained about it being too expensive, he always wanted her to rent a decent car. She would have preferred a Deux Chevaux, which means "two horses," but it looked more like one.

It was nearly six o'clock when Pascale got to St Tropez. She took the D98 after the N98 and D25, and drove along the Route des Plages, using the instructions she'd been given, and twenty minutes later she was still looking for the address, and afraid she'd taken the wrong turn. She was getting hungry, but she wanted to drop her things off at the house before she looked for a place to eat. She wasn't planning to buy groceries until the next day. And as she thought about it, she drove by a pair of crumbling stone pillars, with a set of rusty iron gates. She smiled to herself, thinking how much charm the area had. It felt so good just being back in France. And having passed the gates at full speed, she drove on. But ten minutes later, as she diligently checked the numbers, she realized she'd gone past the address. She turned around and went back, and missed it again. And this time, after she made a U-turn, she inched her way along. She knew the house had to be here somewhere, and the entrance was obviously hidden or extremely discreet. She finally located the number just before it, and stopped the car to look around. As she did so, she found herself at the crumbling stone pillars again. And as she looked more carefully, she saw a small bedraggled sign hanging by a single rusty nail. But there was obviously a mistake. The rusty iron gates were the right street number for their house. And the sign clearly said *Coup de Foudre,* which in French means literally "bolt of lightning," but the more poetic sense is "love at first sight." It was dusk on a magically warm night, and she quietly drove in through the gates.

There was a narrow curving driveway, with unkempt bushes that scraped along her car, and Pascale felt a vague sense of trepidation. This was not the entrance she had expected, or seen in the brochure. Some of the weeds in the middle of the drive were so tall that she had to swerve around them in the car. They were actually more like bushes, and everything was overgrown. It looked like a scene in a horror movie, or a murder mystery, and she laughed at herself, as she came around the last bend, and saw the house. The entrance certainly had been "discreet." You could see nothing of the property from the road. And as the house came into full view, she put her foot full on the brake and stopped. The house was a huge rambling villa, just as the photographs had shown, with handsome French windows, and ivy covering the walls, but the pictures they had looked at must have been taken fifty years before. It looked as though the house had been deserted since then, and was in serious disrepair. She suspected instantly that it was a lot more than two years since the owners had been there, not to mention the photographer who had shot the brochure.

There was a large overgrown front lawn, with grass and weeds that were nearly waist high. There was some old broken lawn furniture strewn around, and an ancient tattered umbrella over a rusty iron table that looked like you'd need a tetanus shot if you ate there. The place looked like a scene in a movie, and for a frantic second she wanted to ask someone if this was a joke. But clearly, it was not. This was their house. And for Pascale at least it was definitely not "love at first sight," it was more like being hit by a bolt of lightning than first love.

"Merde," she said softly, as she sat staring from the car. All she could do now was pray that the photographer had

been more honest in shooting the inside. But it seemed unlikely as she pulled over, got out of the car, and stumbled as she stepped into a hole. The paths around the house were full of potholes, and here and there were little puddles of mud. There were a few flowers that had grown wild. The neat flower beds in the pictures must have disappeared years before. And then it occurred to her to honk the horn. She knew there was a couple waiting for her, and she had written to tell them when she'd come. But despite several long blasts on the horn, there was no response, and she walked gingerly toward the front door.

There was a doorbell and she rang it, but no one came. All she could hear were the sounds of barking dogs, at least two hundred of them from the sound of it, a vast number, and presumably small ones. It was nearly five minutes before anyone came, and then finally she could hear footsteps inside the house. Pascale was standing there, feeling worried, as the door finally opened, and all she could see at first was a vast ball of long, wildly frizzy bleached blond hair. It stood out around the woman's head nearly straight. It looked more like a wig in some wild drugged-out movie of the 1960s, and the face beneath it was small and round. All Pascale could remember now was that the woman's name was Agathe, and she said it with a look of hesitation, trying not to focus unduly on the hair.

"Oui, c'est moi." It is I. It sure was. Who else? She was

wearing a halter top, from which her breasts seemed to explode, there was a vast expanse of stomach, and then the shortest shorts Pascale had ever seen. Her body seemed to be entirely round, like a balloon, with virtually no waist. She was all stomach and breasts, and her only saving grace was that she had good legs, and much to Pascale's chagrin, she was wearing six-inch heels. They were the kind of shoes that in the 1950s had been called FMQs. And she squinted at Pascale with a look of disinterest, as a Gauloise *papier maïs,* with its yellow corn paper, hung from her lips. The smoke rose slowly in a long gray curl, and forced her to close one eye. She was a sight to behold, and whirling around her feet were three frantically yapping little white dogs. Poodles, immaculately trimmed. Unlike their owner, they looked as though they'd been to the hairdresser only minutes before, and each of them was wearing a small pink bow. Pascale continued to stare at the woman, trying unconsciously to determine her age. She was somewhere in her forties, or maybe even fifties, but her skin was smooth on her chubby little face.

Pascale introduced herself, as one of the poodles tried to bite her ankle, and the other attacked her shoe, and Agathe didn't bother telling them to stop.

"They won't hurt you," she reassured Pascale, as she stepped aside, and Pascale caught a glimpse of the living room. It looked like a set from *Bride of Frankenstein*. The furniture was old and battered, you could actually see cobwebs hanging from the ceiling and chandelier, and the supposedly elegant Persian carpets were all threadbare. For an instant, Pascale didn't know what to say, and then she stared at the woman in disbelief.

"Is this the house we rented?" Pascale asked in a voice that sounded more like a croak. She was praying that the woman would tell her the one she had rented was farther up the road. And as Agathe nodded with a chuckle, Pascale's heart sank. By then, the third dog was frantically humping her other shoe. Love at first sight it was not. Except perhaps for the dog.

"It's been closed for a while," Agathe explained blithely. "With a little sunshine tomorrow, it'll look great." It would have taken a lot more than sunshine to make the house look like anything but a tomb. Pascale had never seen anything so grim. The only things she recognized from the photographs were the fireplace and the view, and both were exceptionally pretty, but the rest was a disaster, and she had no idea what to do. The others would be there in two days. All she could do was call the realtor and get their money back. But then what? Where would they stay? At that time of year, all the hotels would be full. And they could hardly go to Italy to stay with her mother. Her mind was racing, and the woman with the blond Afro looked amused.

"The same thing happened to some people from Texas last year."

"What did they do?"

"They sued the realtor and the owner. And they chartered a yacht." At least that was an idea.

"May I see the rest?" Pascale asked weakly, as Agathe nodded, and clicked across the floor again in her high heels. By then the dogs had gotten used to Pascale and only stood there barking, instead of trying to attack her, as Agathe shooed them away. They were unbelievably noisy, and Pascale wanted to kill them as she followed Agathe through the living room.

It was every bit as large as it had looked in the photos, but not a single stick of furniture that had been in the photos was in the room. The dining room was long and bare and empty, with an antique refectory table, dirty canvas chairs, and a chandelier above it that looked as if it were hanging from a thread. Candles had dripped all over the table, and no one had bothered to clean it, seemingly for years. But when Pascale saw the kitchen, she felt as though she had been punched in the stomach, and all she could do was groan. It was absolutely filthy, nothing short of a firehose would have fixed it. Everything was covered with grease and grime, and the air was heavy with the smell of old food. Clearly, Agathe had not been wasting her time cleaning the house.

The bedrooms were slightly better, they were large and

plain and airy, and almost everything in them was white, except for the patches of dirty floral rugs on the floor. But the view from the bedrooms, over the water, was so spectacular that it was conceivable no one would notice or care how sadly the rooms were lacking in decor. It was just remotely possible that if Agathe applied herself, and one filled the room with flowers, one could actually spend a night there. The master suite was the best one, but the others were fairly decent too, just tired and in need of soap, wax, and air.

"You like them?" Agathe asked her, and Pascale hesitated. If they stayed there, which she doubted, there would be a vast amount of work to be done. But she couldn't imagine staying, she knew how spoiled her friends were. Diana liked everything to be perfect, and immaculately clean, and so did Eric, and she knew that neither Robert nor John expected to find this disaster, particularly at the price they'd paid. She just didn't know what to offer them instead, and she hated to give up the hope of spending a month in St Tropez. And she knew that John would never let her live it down. She only thanked God her mother hadn't found it, and she was planning to take on the realtor herself. Maybe she could find them another house.

A glance into the bathrooms confirmed her worst fears. The plumbing was forty or fifty years old, and the dirt everywhere in them had been there for at least as long.

Clearly Agathe didn't do toilets, windows, or floors, or much else. The place was a disgrace. And she couldn't blame the people from Texas for suing the owners and the realtor. She was thinking of doing it herself. And she was suddenly so angry and so disappointed, she wanted to scream.

"C'est une honte," it's a disgrace, she said to Agathe, with a look that was not just French, it was Parisian, and if she had dared, she would have kicked all three barking dogs. "When was the last time this place was cleaned?"

"Only this morning, madame," Agathe said, looking insulted, as Pascale shook her head in barely concealed rage. Clearly no one had cleaned the place in years. "What about the gardener, the man? Your husband. Can't he help you in here?"

"Marius doesn't do domestic work," Agathe said grandly, drawing herself up to her full height, which was barely more than Pascale's, even in six-inch heels. And she was easily three times her girth.

"Well, he may have to, if we have to stay," Pascale warned her, and her eyes were blazing, as she went downstairs to use the phone. There was only one, in the kitchen. Pascale was almost afraid to touch it, it was nearly as greasy as the stove. And when she reached the woman who answered at the realtor's office, she let her have it in a blaze of outraged words. "How could you . . .

how dare you . . ." She threatened lawsuits, mayhem, murder, and told her she had to find them another house, or suites in a hotel. But staying in a hotel wouldn't be nearly as much fun, not to mention the expense. She cringed thinking of John, and lashed into the realtor again. "There is absolutely no way we can stay here, it's unlivable . . . filthy . . . disgusting . . . *déguelace* . . . Have you seen it? What were you thinking? The place hasn't been cleaned in twenty years." And as she said it, Agathe stomped off in a huff with her flock of dogs. Pascale was on the phone with the realtor for half an hour. She promised to come by in the morning, to see how she could help, but she assured Pascale that there wasn't another rental to be had in St Tropez. And she insisted this was a good one, all it needed was a little going-over with a vacuum and some soap. "Are you crazy?" Pascale shrieked at her, no longer in control of her temper. "This place would need an atom bomb. And who is going to do it? My friends are arriving in two days. And they're Americans. This is exactly what they think of France. You've just proven everything that people say about us abroad. Sending us those photographs was dishonest, you robbed us, and this house is a pigsty. We are dishonored," Pascale waxed poetic. "You have betrayed not only me, but France." Pascale wanted to kill her, and the woman kept reassuring her that her friends would love it, and it was really a great house. "Maybe it was once, but not in a very long time."

"I'll send a cleaning team in tomorrow to help them," the realtor tried to calm her, to no avail.

"You be here tomorrow, yourself, at seven o'clock in the morning, with a check refunding us for half the money, or I'm going to sue you. And bring your team with you. You can work here with me for the next two days in fact, and your cleaning team damn well better be good."

"Of course," the realtor said with a slightly supercilious air. She was a friend of the realtor Pascale knew in Paris, and Pascale had already assured her that unless she wrought a miracle, her reputation with the agency in Paris would be instantly as over the hill as the house. "I'll do everything I can to help you."

"Bring a lot of people, a lot of cleaning equipment, and a hell of a lot of soap."

"Whatever I can do to be of service," the realtor said haughtily.

"Thank you," Pascale said through clenched teeth, trying to control her temper, but it was a little late for that. She had let the woman have it, and she deserved it. She had misled them completely, to the point of fraud. And as Pascale wandered out of the kitchen, she jumped. She was staring at a man who looked ten feet tall. He was tall and thin and scary, with a long beard and long hair, and he was wearing American denim overalls, with no shirt and a pair of patent leather dress shoes. He looked like a homeless person who had wandered into the house. And with a final sinking of her stomach, Pascale guessed who he was. He was carrying one of the French poodles, still barking, as he lovingly adjusted the pink bow. He could only be Agathe's husband, Marius. When Pascale asked him, he bowed.

"At your service, madame. *Bienvenue.*" Welcome. Hardly. She wanted to kick him in the shins for the state the grounds were in. He was supposed to be the gardener and chauffeur.

"You have a lot of work to do," Pascale said bluntly. "Do you have a lawn mower?" He looked blank for an instant, as though she had asked him for some obscure and rarely heard of tool.

"Yes, I believe so."

"Then I want you to start cutting the grass at six A.M. It will take you all day to clean up these grounds."

"Ah, but madame . . . so much charm . . ."

"Weeds are not charming," Pascale said, glaring at him, as he stroked the dog. "The garden is not charming. And the front lawn is a disgrace. I am not asking you, I am telling you to do something about it. And after you do that, we are going to need your help in the house. We have a lot of work to do." She saw a look pass between Marius and Agathe, and they did not look pleased.

"He has a bad back," Agathe explained, "he cannot exert himself. It's very tiring for him." He was all of forty-five years old, and he looked more lazy than tired. In fact, Pascale suspected that he was either drunk or stoned. He had a kind of goony smile, and a dazed expression, and when he bowed to her for the third time, he looked unsteady on his feet. But Pascale didn't give a damn. She was going to pour coffee into him, if she had to, or give him speed. He *had* to do the work. For the moment there was no one else. And God only knew who would be on the realtor's cleaning "team."

"We have two days," Pascale said ominously, "before the others arrive. And when they do, this house *will* be clean." It was obvious, as far as they were concerned, she had lived in America for too long. But no matter what they thought, she was determined to get what she needed out of them. And as she looked at them, she drew herself up to her full height, and she was every inch the ballet mistress, and the tyrant she knew she would have to be. "Do you cook?" she asked Agathe then. The brochure had said she did.

"Not much," Agathe answered with a shrug, dropping ashes all over her chest. She brushed them away so they didn't get on the dog she was clutching to her. The third one was on the floor and yapping as loudly as it could.

Pascale had a massive headache by then. And as she contemplated a meal prepared by Agathe, she decided it was just as well she didn't cook. She could do that much herself. And they could go out to the restaurants in St Tropez, if John was willing to.

"Would you like me to bring in your bags?" Marius asked pleasantly, exhaling wine fumes at her. He was like a dragon breathing fire as she looked at him. She wanted to tell him that she would prefer to go to a hotel. But she realized that if she did, if she could even get a room, the work would never get done. These two needed a watchful eye, a firm hand, and a stick of dynamite to get them moving. And putting the dogs to sleep would have helped. But they were the least of her problems, as she handed Marius the keys to her car.

A moment later, he was back with her bags. "The master suite, madame?" he asked, holding two of her bags, with his long stringy hair, and his overalls and ridiculous patent leather shoes. She wanted to laugh just looking at him, the whole situation was absurd.

"Yes, that will do." They could always give the room to the Morrisons later, but for right now, she thought she might as well. He brought her bags up to the master bedroom for her, and with a look of despair, she sat down in the only chair. And as she did, the springs gave way, and she sagged nearly to the floor. They left her after a few minutes, and she just sat there, staring out the window.

The view was so perfect, and the house was a nightmare. She wasn't sure whether to laugh or cry. She thought for a minute about calling Diana, but what could she tell her? She hated to disappoint her and Eric, and Robert, and she didn't even dare think of what John would say. She just prayed he wouldn't call, because she knew he would hear it in her voice. But mercifully, she knew how busy he was before going away. All she could do now was try to make it up to them, and get the place in shape. It would take a miracle to get it done in two days. And as the sun set over the water, she leaned her head back in the ancient chair. She was utterly exhausted, and she had a splitting headache, and for the next two days, she knew she would have to make magic. It was a hell of a beginning to their month in St Tropez, but Pascale refused to be defeated. No matter what, she was going to make it work.

6

PASCALE SET HER ALARM for five-thirty, and when she got up, she put on jeans and a T-shirt, and went down to the kitchen, to see if she could find some coffee. She found just enough to make herself a *café filtre*, and with a look of very Gallic despair, she sat on an ancient kitchen chair, and lit a cigarette. She was sitting there smoking, wondering if she'd have to wake them, when one of the dogs ran into the kitchen and barked at her. And two seconds later, Agathe appeared, wearing an apron over a red bikini, from which her round ball of a body seemed to ooze.

"You wear that to work in?" Pascale asked with a look of astonished dismay. But nothing surprised her anymore. If anything, her vast bleached blond Afro seemed larger than the day before. She had even put on lipstick to match her bikini, and the heels she wore today were higher, as her three poodles clustered around her feet like so many furry little white balls. And of course, they started barking the instant they saw Pascale.

"Do you suppose we could put them somewhere while we're working?" Pascale asked Agathe, as she poured herself a second cup of coffee, and realized she hadn't eaten since lunch the day before. She would have given her right arm for a croissant from her mother's kitchen, but in this one, she had discovered, the cupboards were bare. And she had no time to go to the store. She wanted to get Agathe and Marius started. At least Agathe appeared at the hour she'd requested, that was something. And Marius came along five minutes later. He said he had found the lawn mower, although it was pretty old.

But at least when Pascale saw it, she was relieved to see it had a motor, and she told him to start it and keep mowing, until he had cleared everything in sight.

"Everything?" He looked astonished when she nodded, and she figured it would keep him busy for hours. It was not a prospect he enjoyed. Agathe had gone to put the dogs in their bedroom behind the kitchen, and she had come back with rags and soaps and a feather duster, and she began waving it like a wand somewhere in midair, until Pascale took it from her and handed her the rag and some cleaning products, and suggested she get to work in the kitchen. Pascale was going to do the living room herself.

First she rolled the rugs up and put them in a closet. The floors were better looking than the threadbare rugs.

And then she beat the cushions of the couch, and the curtains, and vacuumed everything in sight. She was choking from the dust as she did it, but things started to look a little better by the time she was fluffing up the cushions, and growling at the stains. She waxed the tables, used newspaper on the windows, as her grandmother had taught her, and cleaned absolutely every surface, and then she waxed the floors. The room did not look anything like the pictures, but it was looking better when the realtor and her "team" of minions arrived, looking hot and bored. They were all kids, the realtor had recruited them that morning to do whatever Pascale required.

Pascale had another heated conversation with the realtor, who actually agreed to return half what they had paid, and Pascale knew that John would be pleased. But he'd be even more so, as would the others, if she could also get the house clean. And then she had an idea.

She went upstairs to her suitcase and brought out a stack of brightly colored shawls she had brought with her. She tucked them in over the tired stained upholstery, and the room looked entirely different when she'd finished. The windows were clean, the drapes had been pulled back, all the cobwebs had disappeared, the floors shone like honey, and the brightly covered couches and chairs made the room look simple but festive. All it needed now were flowers and candles and some brighter lightbulbs.

The cleaning team was hard at work in the kitchen,

and Pascale had sent Agathe off to do the bathrooms, and scrub them until they shone, while Marius worked in the hot sun mowing the lawns. And when she checked on him, he wasn't pleased, but what he was doing made a huge difference. There were old broken lawn chairs emerging from the tall grasses, and two-legged wooden tables that had all but disintegrated, and she made him haul them all away. The weeds were slowly disappearing, and the wildflowers that had grown along the edges of the lawn had a certain charm.

It was eight o'clock at night before they were all finished, and the realtor looked at Pascale in stupefaction. It wasn't perfect, and it didn't look like the pictures, but it was a hell of an improvement over what Pascale had found there the day before. The kitchen still looked somewhat depressing, and the stove was ancient, but at least everything was clean.

Pascale was exhausted, she had been working for fourteen hours, but it was worth it. The others might be startled when they saw it, but at least they wouldn't run screaming out the door. The realtor had brought cheese and fruit and pâté, and Pascale had nibbled a little, but she had hardly eaten all day. All she wanted was to get it finished, and the realtor promised, when she left, to return with her workers the next day. And Marius would have to do more mowing. Agathe had clucked in sympathy all day, and if possible, she looked even wilder by the time she finished. The red bikini was sagging and drooping, the high-heeled sandals had vanished, and her hair looked as though she had stuck a finger in a socket, and mercifully, Pascale hadn't seen or heard the dogs all day.

Pascale was sitting in the kitchen, staring into space in exhaustion, picking at the remains of the pâté, when the phone rang and she started. And then grabbed it. It was John calling from the office, and he sounded happy and excited. They hadn't seen each other in six weeks, and he was delighted to be seeing her in two days.

"Well, how is it? Is it terrific?" he asked, sounding enthusiastic, and she closed her eyes, trying to decide what to say.

"It's a little different from the pictures," she said, wondering what he'd say when he saw it. At least it was clean now, and it looked a lot better, but it was certainly no palace, and it bore very little resemblance to the elegant photographs they'd seen.

"Is it better?" John asked, sounding elated, and Pascale laughed as she shook her head. She was so tired, she could barely think.

"Not exactly. It's just different. A little more informal maybe."

"That sounds great." *Great* was not exactly the word Pascale would have used to describe the house called Love at First Sight, but she had done the best she could. "Have you talked to the others?"

"No, I've been too busy," she said, sounding exhausted, and John laughed at what she'd said.

"Doing what? Lying on the beach?" He had envisioned her swimming and sunbathing all day, not scrubbing floors and bathroom walls.

"No, I was just busy organizing the house."

"Why don't you just relax for a change?" She would have loved it, but if she had, he would have had a stroke when he walked through the door.

"Maybe tomorrow," she said vaguely, through a yawn.

"Well, I'll see you the day after that."

"I can hardly wait," she smiled, thinking of him, as she sat in the dilapidated kitchen. As she sat there, she could see a spot of grease they'd missed on the stove.

"Get some sleep, or you'll be exhausted when we arrive."

"Don't worry. I will. Have a safe trip." After they hung up, she turned out the lights, and went up to bed. She had made Agathe change the sheets, the others had been gray and frayed, and she had finally found a pair for each bed that looked relatively unused. The towels looked tired too, but at least now they were clean. She fell asleep almost the minute her head touched the pillow, and she slept until the sun came up the next day. The shades didn't roll down, and the shutters were broken too. But she didn't mind the sun filling the room.

And she worked just as hard that day. The workers the realtor had provided were worn out by then, and grumbling, but Pascale managed to keep them there all afternoon. And when she went outside to see what Marius had done, the front lawn looked impeccable, and all the broken lawn furniture had disappeared. What was left was serviceable, though in dire need of a coat of paint. She wondered if she had time for Marius to tackle that too. But when she looked for him, she found him in his room, snoring and sound asleep, with all three dogs draped over him, and three empty beer bottles on his bed. It was obvious that, for the moment at least, she wasn't going to get much more work out of him. And Agathe was wearing out too.

At five o'clock, Pascale drove into St Tropez, and came back with the car full. She had bought candles and flowers, and huge vases to put them in, and arrangements of dried flowers too. She had bought three more colorful shawls to use in the living room, and three cans of white paint for Marius to tackle the lawn furniture the next day. And by the time she was through, at nine o'clock, every inch of the house was immaculate, the lawns had been mowed, the weeds pulled, and there were flowers and magazines in every room. She had bought wonderful French soaps, and spare towels for all of them, and every room of the villa had been magically transformed. It may not have been love at first sight, but it was drastically improved.

She couldn't even imagine what they'd say when they saw the house now. It looked better to her, but it was still not what any of them had thought it would be. And she was afraid they would all be angry at her. But there wasn't much more she could do, without a house painter, a contractor, and a decorator. And when she finally went down to see the boat at the dock that night, she wondered if it would even sail. It looked as though it had been tied up for years, and the sails looked tattered and stained, but she knew that if there was any hope at all, Robert and Eric would get it under sail.

She fell into bed exhausted again that night, but with a sense of accomplishment. She was enormously relieved that she had had the foresight to come down two days before their lease began. If she hadn't, she was sure the others would never have stayed, and now she thought they would. At least, she hoped they would. She didn't want to give up the month in St Tropez.

She slept like a rock that night, and it was ten o'clock when she woke up the next day, the sun was streaming into the room, and the flowers she had put on tables everywhere added splashes of color and life to the room. She made herself coffee from the supplies she'd bought, and ate a *pain au chocolat* as she read an old copy of *Paris Match,* and then moved on to *The International Herald Tribune.* When she was in France, she liked reading *Le Monde* too, but John always insisted on having the *Herald Tribune,* and she had bought it for him the day before.

As Pascale put her dishes in the sink, Agathe came into the room, wearing electric green bicycle pants, and a white halter top you could just barely see through. She looked like one of her French poodles with her hair all puffed out, and she was wearing harlequin sunglasses with rhinestones at either end, and frighteningly high gold platform shoes.

"Nice day," Agathe commented, rinsing Pascale's cup out with a lazy hand. "What time do your friends arrive?" she inquired disinterestedly, as though it was of no great consequence to her.

"Not until late this afternoon. I'd like Marius to drive to the airport with me, with the truck. I don't have room in the trunk of my car for their things."

"He hurt his back yesterday," Agathe said accusingly, as her left eye squinted at her employer for the month. Her right eye was closed to accommodate the Gauloise that seemed to be eternally glued to her lips.

"Can he still drive?" Pascale inquired, watching her, wondering whether or not to say something about her clothes.

"Maybe" was all Agathe would say. And Pascale understood what was required. She went discreetly to her handbag and took out five hundred francs for each of them.

They had worked hard, surely harder than either of them had worked in years. And Agathe looked pleased. Pascale had understood. She had meant to give them something anyway. "I think he'll be all right to drive. What time do you want to leave?"

"Three o'clock. Their plane arrives at five. We'll be back by dinnertime." Pascale had already planned to leave dinner on the stove. None of them would want to go out the first night. They'd be tired from the trip, and want to settle in.

She even got Marius to paint some of the lawn furniture that day, for an extra five hundred francs, and by the time they left, the house actually looked okay. She had wrought a miracle, and even Agathe commented just before they left, and said that the place looked great. She was surprised Pascale had stayed, and not gone to a hotel. No one had actually stayed in the house in years.

"We did good work, didn't we?" Pascale looked pleased, and Agathe's dogs yapped around her feet as she helped herself to a beer and took a long swig. And when they left for the airport, she waved at Pascale as though they were old friends. She was wearing a shocking pink see-through blouse, with a black bra, and bright pink shorts, and her favorite red FMQ shoes. She was quite a fashion plate, and Pascale had decided not to tackle her wardrobe with her. The others could live with it, although perhaps not with the barking dogs. Pascale had asked her to keep them in her room as much as she could. Pascale said her husband was allergic to them, which he was, not to their fur, but most assuredly to their noise.

It was a long hot drive back to Nice from St Tropez, and when they got to the airport, Pascale bought a glass of orange juice, and she saw Marius buy a beer. He was wearing his overalls and patent leather shoes again, obviously his dress uniform, as she waited for the plane to get in. She had never been as tired in her life. She really needed the vacation now.

The flight from New York had gone smoothly, and John had flown with the Morrisons, although he didn't sit with them. They had flown business, as they always did, and he had flown coach. Eric had teased him about it when he walked back to visit him, and they'd chatted for a while, and then John walked him back to his seat. Diana had been reading quietly, and John saw an odd look pass between them. It was a chill he had never seen before, but neither of them said anything, and he went back to his own seat to sleep. He was excited about seeing Pascale. For all their bickering, he was still very much in love with her, after twenty-five years. She kept his life interesting, and she was so passionate about everything, whether it was lovemaking or arguing. The apartment in New York had seemed lonely and lifeless without her for the past six weeks.

"John tells me that Pascale says the house looks great,"

Eric said as he sat down next to Diana again, and for a long moment, she didn't answer him, and kept her eyes on her book. "Did you hear what I said?" he asked quietly, and she lifted her eyes to his. It had been touch and go for the past several weeks as to whether or not she would come. He was glad she had decided to in the end, and relieved. Things had been tense between them for the past month. And the stress they'd been through showed on Diana's face, if not his.

"I heard what you said," she confirmed expressionlessly. With no one else they knew around them, she didn't have to make any pretense. "I'm glad Pascale likes the house." Her eyes looked dead as she spoke.

"I hope you will too," he said gently. He wanted this to be a good time for them. They needed that desperately, and he was hoping that a month in France would solidify the bond between them again. They had always had so much in common, loved doing the same things, enjoyed the same people, and genuinely admired each other.

"I don't know how long I'm going to stay," she reiterated the mantra she'd been saying for the past two weeks. "I'll see."

"Running away isn't going to solve anything. We'll have fun with the others, and it'll do us both good," he said hopefully, but Diana looked anything but convinced.

"Having 'fun' isn't going to solve anything either. It's not about 'fun.' " There were far bigger issues at stake. He had put their life on the line and their marriage in jeopardy, and Diana had not yet made up her mind what she was going to do about it. Several times in the past weeks, she had come to a decision, and then changed her mind again. She didn't want to be hasty. But she wasn't sure she could forgive him for what he'd done. He had wounded her mortally, and shaken her faith, not only in him, but in herself. She felt flawed now, and undesirable, and suddenly far older than she looked. She didn't know if she would ever feel the same way about him again.

"Diana, can we try and put this behind us now?" he asked quietly. But it was easy for him to say, far easier than it was for her.

"Thanks for asking me," she said sarcastically, and picked up her book again. "Now that I know what I have to do, I'm sure everything will be fine." There were tears in her eyes as she pretended to read the book she held, but her mind had been drifting for the past hour, and she had no idea what she'd read. She just held the book so he wouldn't talk to her. There was nothing left she wanted to say. In the past agonizing weeks, they had said it all.

"Diana . . . don't be like that . . . ," he said, and she pretended not to hear at first, and then turned her head to look at him. All the grief she felt was written all over her face.

"How do you expect me to be, Eric? Amused? Indifferent? Casual? Cheerful, maybe? . . . Oh that's right, I'm supposed to be the doting, adoring, understanding wife. Well, maybe I can't." Her voice caught on the last words.

"Why don't you just give us a chance? Let the dust settle while we're here. It's been a tough time, for both of us. . . ." Before he could say anything more, she cut him off, and stood up.

"Forgive me if I'm not too sympathetic about how 'tough' this has been for you. That's not exactly my take on it. Nice try." And with that, she climbed over him, and disappeared down the aisle to get away from him and go for a walk. She didn't want to discuss it with him again. They'd said enough in the past month. She didn't want to hear about it again, his excuses, his promises, his apologies, his rationale for what he'd done. She didn't even want to be there with him, and was sorry she had come. She had only come on the trip so as not to disappoint their friends. She walked all the way back to where John was sitting, and when she spotted him, she saw that he was sound asleep. She stood looking out the porthole in the door at the back of the plane, thinking of the state their marriage was in. She was devastated, she had never thought it would come to this. Everything they had shared and believed, all the trust she had always felt for Eric seemed shattered beyond repair. And when she went back to her seat, she said nothing to him, and they didn't speak to each other again for the rest of the flight.

Their flight got in on time, and Pascale beamed when she saw John, with the Morrisons walking right behind him. They looked tired, and were less talkative than usual, but all four of them chatted animatedly about the house once they were in the car, with Marius following in the truck with their bags. They were a little startled when they saw Marius, and she tried to prepare them for Agathe on the drive back to St Tropez, but it was difficult to describe her adequately, particularly in the red bikini and FMQs.

"Doesn't she wear a uniform?" John inquired. He had somehow envisioned a French couple in white dress and white jacket, serving lunch impeccably in the elegant villa. But the portrait Pascale was painting for them was definitely different from what he'd had in mind.

"Not exactly," she answered. "They're a little eccentric, but they work hard." And they drank a lot. And their dogs never stopped barking, she could have added, but didn't. "I hope you like the house," Pascale said nervously, when they finally got back to St Tropez at seven-thirty.

"I'm sure we're going to love it," Eric said confidently

as she drove between the crumbling pillars, and passed through the gates.

"It's a little more rustic than we thought," Pascale said, as she rattled down the potholed driveway. John already looked a little surprised, and she noticed that the Morrisons were sitting in the backseat in total silence, which wasn't like them. But they were probably tired, and subdued by her subtle warnings. And as she pulled up in front of the house, John stared.

"It needs a coat of paint, or an overhaul or something, doesn't it?"

"It needs a lot more than that, but at least it's clean now," Pascale said humbly.

"Wasn't the house clean when you arrived?" Diana asked, with a look of amazement.

"Not exactly." And then Pascale laughed. There was no point keeping it from them. Now that they were here, it seemed better to tell them the truth. "It was a pigsty when I arrived. I've spent two days cleaning it up with a team of ten people. But the good news is we got half our money back, because they really misled us." John looked thrilled by what she had just said. To him, it was almost like getting a free vacation, and he loved that.

"Is it really awful, Pascale?" Diana looked suddenly worried, and Eric was ready to reassure her. The last thing he wanted was for Diana to leave.

"No, it's not awful, but everything in it is pretty old

and battered, and there's not much furniture. And the kitchen is out of the Middle Ages," Pascale said honestly.

"Oh, so what? Who cares?" John laughed. Now that he knew he'd gotten half his money back, he already loved it. It had been the right thing to say to him before he saw it up close.

And as they walked inside, Diana gasped. She was startled by how bare and ramshackle it was, but she had to admit that Pascale's shawls on the furniture were a clever touch. She knew that the upholstery must have been a disaster for her to do that. But once they looked around, they decided it wasn't so bad. Not what they had hoped for, of course, but at least Pascale had prepared them. And when she told them what it had looked like when she'd arrived, and what she'd done, they were impressed and grateful for her efforts.

"It's a good thing you got here before we did," Eric said as they glanced into the kitchen. It was spotless, but as antiquated as Pascale had already warned.

"How the hell did they ever get those pictures?" John said with a look of astonishment.

"Apparently they took them about forty years ago, in the sixties."

"How dishonest of them, that's disgusting," Eric said with a look of disapproval, but he seemed satisfied with the house. It was comfortable and clean, and very informal, not the luxurious villa they had been expecting, but thanks to Pascale and her efforts on their behalf, it had a certain charm, particularly with all the flowers she had put around, and the candles. She offered to give up the master suite to the Morrisons, but when they realized all she'd done for them, they insisted that she and John keep it.

"I just did it so you wouldn't hate me," she admitted, and they all laughed as John went to find a bottle of wine, and ran smack into Agathe, standing in the kitchen. She was wearing white shorts, and the top of her red bikini, with her red high-heeled sandals, and he stood and stared at her for an instant. As usual, she had one eye closed and was smoking a Gauloise.

"Bonjour," he said awkwardly. He had learned that much French the first time he'd gone to meet Pascale's mother. Agathe smiled at him, and an instant later, Marius appeared, with the flock of barking dogs just behind him. "Oh Jesus" was all John could think of to say, as one of them grabbed his pants leg, and in less than five seconds, managed to chew through it.

Marius opened the wine for him, and Agathe disappeared with the dogs again, as John looked a little dazed, and went upstairs, carrying the bottle of red wine and four glasses.

"I just met the hounds of the Baskervilles and Tina Turner's evil twin." Pascale laughed at the description, and saw something sorrowful flit across Diana's face, but when she glanced at Eric, she saw nothing. She wondered if Diana had been thinking of Anne, and how much she had wanted to come here. It had crossed her mind too, when she arrived, but from then on she had been too busy to think about her. And she was sure it would hit Robert too. Anne was still sorely missed, and it was impossible not to think of her enthusiasm about spending a month here.

"Have you seen the boat?" Eric asked hopefully, as John poured them all wine.

"I have," Pascale confessed. "It dates back to Robinson Crusoe. I hope you can still sail it."

"I'm sure we'll be able to get her going." He glanced at his wife then with a smile, and Diana said nothing.

Pascale cooked dinner for them that night. Agathe had already set the dining room table, and she offered to serve, but Pascale said she could manage without her. And afterward, when she and Diana were clearing the dishes, and John and Eric were smoking cigars in the garden, Pascale couldn't help looking at her and asking her a question. She was worried about her.

"Are you all right? You've seemed upset to me for a while, and in New York, I kept thinking you were just tired. Are you okay, Diana?"

There was a long pause as her friend looked at her, started to nod, and then shook her head emphatically. She sat down at the ancient kitchen table, as tears began rolling slowly down her cheeks, and she looked up at Pascale, heartbroken, and no longer able or willing to conceal her sorrow from her friend.

"What's wrong? . . . oh poor thing . . . What happened?" Pascale put an arm around her as she asked her, and Diana wiped her eyes with her apron.

She couldn't even bring herself to say the words. She leaned against Pascale for a minute, as Pascale held her like a child, and wondered what had happened to so desperately upset her. She had never seen Diana like that.

"Are you sick?" Diana shook her head, but continued to say nothing. All she could do was blow her nose in the paper towel Pascale had just handed her. "It's not you and Eric, is it?" Pascale meant the question to be rhetorical, but as soon as she saw Diana's face, Pascale knew it was. Diana sat and stared at her for a long moment, and then finally nodded. "It isn't! How can that be?"

"I don't know how it can be. I've been asking him the same question for the last month."

"What happened?" Pascale looked stunned, and Diana looked devastated.

"He's been having an affair with one of his patients," she said, and blew her nose again. In a way, it was a relief to tell Pascale. She hadn't told a soul since he had admitted it to her. It was her solitary ugly secret.

"Are you sure you're not imagining it? I just can't believe that."

"Well, it's true. He told me. I knew something was wrong for about two months, but I didn't know what, and four weeks ago, he admitted it to me. Katherine's baby got croup and had to go to the hospital in the middle of the night, so I called Eric to ask him to meet them in the emergency room, and they told me he hadn't been there all night. He had told me he was doing a delivery. He even called me and told me he'd be stuck there until morning and would go straight to the office afterward. All of a sudden, I realized that most of the time he's been telling me he was at the hospital at night, he wasn't."

"Eric?" Pascale's voice cracked as she said it. To Pascale, he had always seemed like the perfect husband. Easygoing, good-humored, considerate, kind to his wife, the ideal husband and father. "Is he in love with her?"

"He says he's not sure. He said he stopped seeing her a few days ago, and maybe he did, she's been calling him at home every night. I think he's very upset about it. He says she's a nice woman. She was one of his patients, and her husband deserted her right after she had her baby. He felt sorry for her. And she must be very pretty, she's a model."

"How old is she?" Pascale asked, looking agonized for

her. It was every woman's worst nightmare. Diana looked ravaged by what she'd told Pascale.

"She's thirty," Diana said, looking heartbroken. "I'm old enough to be her mother. She's the same age as Katherine. I feel about six hundred years old. He'd probably be better off with her." And then she looked up at Pascale with stricken eyes, "I don't think I'll ever trust him again. I'm not even sure I can stay married to him now."

"You can't do that," Pascale said, looking horrified. "You can't divorce him. Not after all this time. That would be just terrible. If he stopped seeing her, then it's over. He'll forget about her," Pascale said, looking hopeful, but still desperately sorry for her friend.

"Maybe he will forget her. But I won't," Diana said honestly. "Every time I look at him, I'll know he betrayed me. I hate him for it."

"That's understandable," Pascale said sympathetically. "But it happens to people sometimes. Maybe it could even have happened to you. If he ended it with this girl, you have to try to forgive him for it. Diana, you can't divorce him. It will ruin your life, as well as his. You love each other."

"Apparently not as much as I thought. At least he doesn't." There was nothing in her eyes of forgiveness, only anger and hurt and disappointment, and Pascale felt so sorry for her.

"What does he say about it?"

"That he's sorry. That it'll never happen again. That he regretted it the minute he did it, but he still did it for three months, and it might have gone on longer if Katherine's baby hadn't gotten sick that night. He might even have left me for her." Diana only cried harder as she said the words.

"He can't be that stupid." But he was handsome and looked terrific for his age, and he dealt with women all day long. He had more opportunities than most men to meet women. And anything was possible, even for a man as responsible and trustworthy as Eric. But she could see in Diana's eyes what it had done to her. Pascale was amazed she had actually come on this vacation, and asked her about it.

"I wasn't going to after I found out, but he begged me to come. And now he says he can only stay for two weeks, and if he goes, I'm going to think he's with her every minute."

"Maybe you should believe him, that it's over," Pascale said quietly, but Diana looked furious about it.

"Why should I believe him? He lied to me. How can I possibly be expected to trust him?" She had a point, and Pascale didn't know what to answer. But it broke her heart to think of them ending their marriage. "I just don't think I can stay married to him, Pascale. It will never be the same for me again, and I probably shouldn't have come on this vacation. I told him I was going to call a lawyer before we left, and he asked me to wait at least until this trip is over. But I don't think it'll make any difference." It was a heavy burden to be taking with them on the trip, like a set of lead luggage. And it didn't bode well for the vacation. "Would you stay married to John if he cheated on you?" Diana asked her, looking her in the eye with a bitter expression. She didn't even seem like the same woman. She had always been so carefree and so happy, as had Eric. And they had such a great relationship. Of the three couples, Pascale had always thought they had the best marriage, or maybe Robert and Anne did. She and John had always had their differences, and they argued a lot more than the others. And now Anne was gone, and Diana was talking about divorcing Eric. It didn't bear thinking.

"I don't know what I would do," Pascale said honestly. "I'm sure I'd want to kill him." John always talked a lot about women, but Pascale never thought he did anything about it. In fact, she was sure he didn't. He just liked the aura it gave him. But it was all talk and bravado in his case. "I think I'd have to give it a lot of thought before I did anything, and maybe try to trust him again. People do these things sometimes, Diana."

"Don't be so French about it," Diana growled at her, and then started to cry again. She was absolutely miserable, and she was still sorry she had come on this vacation. Every time she looked at him, it upset her. She didn't know how she was going to get through the month, or even another day, with him.

"Maybe the French are right about some things," Pascale said gently. "You have to give it a lot of thought before you do anything you'll regret later."

"He should have done that, before he slept with that woman," Diana said angrily. And it seemed particularly cruel that the woman was so much younger. It made Diana feel suddenly old and unattractive. He had hurt her in the most painful way possible, and she didn't know how she was going to live through it, or if their marriage would survive.

"Have you told anyone?" Pascale asked cautiously.

"Only you," Diana answered. "I've been too ashamed to. I don't know why I should feel embarrassed, but I do. It makes me feel like less of a person, as though I wasn't enough for him." She truly looked devastated.

"Diana, you know that's not true. He just did something very stupid. And I'm sure he's embarrassed too," Pascale said, trying to be fair to both of them. "I think it was brave of you to come here." She actually admired her for it, although it was obvious Diana wasn't looking forward to being there. She was too distraught to care about the trip.

"I didn't want to let you down," Diana said sadly, "or Robert. I know how hard it will be for him to come here. I felt I owed it to him too. I came more for him than for Eric."

"Maybe it will do you both good to be here," Pascale said hopefully. But they needed a lot more than a vacation on the Riviera. Their marriage needed major surgery, not Band-Aids.

"I don't think I'll ever forgive him for it," Diana said, crying again.

"Not yet certainly. But maybe in time," Pascale said wisely. She put an arm around her friend then, and they hugged each other, and after a while they went back to the living room to join their husbands. And when the men came back inside after their cigars, Pascale could see now the chasm between Diana and Eric. They looked at each other as though they had lost each other, and Pascale's heart ached for them.

She was still looking depressed about it when she and John went upstairs to their bedroom, and he noticed it immediately, which was unusual for him. Sometimes he was far less perceptive about her. "Is something wrong?" He wondered if he had inadvertently done or said something to upset her.

"No, I was just thinking." She didn't want to say anything to him, unless Diana gave her permission. She didn't want to violate her confidence, and she had meant to ask her if she could tell him, but she hadn't.

"What about?" John asked, looking concerned. Pascale really looked worried.

"Nothing important. What to make for lunch tomorrow." She lied to him, but only to protect Diana and Eric's secret.

"I don't believe you. Is it something big?"

"Sort of."

"I think I know what it is. Eric just told me he and Diana were having problems." John looked upset about it too.

"Did he say what kind of problems?"

"No. Men aren't usually that specific. He just said they had hit a rough spot in the marriage."

"She wants to divorce him," Pascale said, looking grief-stricken. "That would be just awful. For both of them."

"Is it another woman?" John asked, and she nodded. John looked as distressed as she did.

"He says it's over, but Diana says she's too hurt to forgive him."

"I hope they'll work it out," John said, looking concerned. "They've got thirty-two years behind them. That counts for something." He pulled her into his arms then, with a gentle look, which was unlike him. Most of the time he was gruff and blustery, but beneath it, she knew he loved her. "I missed you," he said gently.

"I missed you too," she smiled at him, and then he kissed her. And a moment later, he turned the lights out and took her in his arms. It had been six weeks since they'd seen each other, a long time in any marriage, but he knew how much being in Paris meant to her, and he would never have deprived her of it. She lived for her time there every year.

They lay in each other's arms for a long time that night, after they made love, with a full moon shining in their bedroom window. And after he fell asleep, she lay next to him and watched him, wondering how she would feel if he ever did to her what Eric had just done to Diana. She knew how devastated she would be. Just as much so as Diana. And all she could think as she looked at him was how lucky she was to have him. He was all she needed and wanted, and always had been.

7

THE NEXT MORNING, as Pascale made breakfast for all of them, John arrived in the kitchen looking somewhat panicked. He was holding a brass handle in one hand, as Agathe drifted through, wearing a leopard bikini, platform shoes, and wearing a Walkman as she carried a dustbin and sang to herself loudly. John stopped long enough to stare at her in disbelief, as Pascale continued to scramble eggs, looking totally unconcerned by the vision Agathe presented. She had gotten used to her by then, and seemed entirely oblivious to her appearance.

"The toilet is flooding!" John announced, waving the brass handle at her. "What am I supposed to do about it?"

"I don't know. Can't you deal with it? I'm cooking." Pascale looked vaguely amused as he continued to wave the brass handle in her direction. "Why don't you call Marius and get him to help you?" she suggested, and he rolled his eyes in irritation.

"How do I know where to find him? And how do I tell him what happened?"

"Just show him," Pascale said as she waved at Agathe to catch her attention. She was still singing, but she finally took the Walkman off while Pascale explained the problem. But she didn't look surprised, she just took the brass handle from John and waddled off to find her husband. He appeared minutes later with a bucket, a mop, and a plunger. He was wearing shorts and a see-through T-shirt, and he looked excruciatingly hung over.

Agathe was telling her by then it happened all the time, and wasn't a big problem, and just as she said it, a thin stream of water began trickling through the kitchen ceiling. And both John and Pascale looked up in panic. He left at a dead run to return to the scene of the crime, and Marius followed him more slowly, as Agathe put her Walkman back on, and sang loudly as she set the table.

Eric and Diana walked into the kitchen then, and Eric looked startled when he saw Agathe in her leopard bikini and apron. "That's a look," he said circumspectly, and Diana burst into laughter.

"Does she always look like that?" Diana asked, as Pascale turned off the stove and smiled at her. She was pleased to see that they both looked a little more relaxed and rested than they had the night before.

"More or less. Sometimes she wears more, sometimes less, but it's usually the same kind of outfit. But she's a pretty good cleaner. She helped me get the place in shape before you got here."

"It looks cool, anyway," Eric said, as he picked a peach from the bowl on the kitchen table. The fruit Pascale had bought was delicious. "Is it raining in here, or do we have a problem?" Eric asked, looking up at the steady stream of water coming from the ceiling.

"John says the toilet is flooding," Pascale said as Eric nodded, and she served the eggs. A few minutes later, John joined them, looking harassed and a little frantic.

"There are two inches of water on the bathroom floor. I had Marius turn off the water till he calls the plumber."

"How did you manage to tell him all that?" Pascale looked impressed. In twenty-five years, he had barely said ten words of French to her mother, most of it *bonjour* and *au revoir*, and *merci*, and only when he truly had to.

"I used to play charades when I was in high school," he said, diving into the eggs, as Marius walked in and put a bucket under the stream of water coming through the ceiling. It seemed to be coming faster and harder, but he looked unconcerned, as he disappeared again and Agathe followed.

"Did you sleep well?" Pascale asked Eric over their eggs. And she poured them all steaming cups of strong coffee.

"Perfectly," Eric answered, with a glance at Diana. They seemed not to be speaking to each other, or at least not more than they absolutely had to. And there was a definite sense of tension between them, and as soon as they finished eating, Pascale suggested to Diana that they go to the market. John wanted to stay back and see the plumber, and Eric announced that he was going to check out the sailboat and see if it would sail.

It was an easy morning for all of them, the weather was spectacular, and Diana and Pascale chatted on the way to the market. Pascale commented that Eric seemed to be trying to make an effort to be nice to her, and Diana nodded and stared out the window.

"He is," she admitted to her friend, "but I'm not sure it'll make a difference."

"Maybe you should just see what happens on the vacation. The time away may do you both good, if you let it."

"And then what? We forget it all, and pretend it never happened? How do you think I could do that?" Diana looked annoyed at the suggestion.

"I'm not sure I could either," Pascale said honestly, "I'd probably kill John if he did something like that. But maybe that's what you have to do to fix it."

"Why do *I* have to fix it?" Diana asked, sounding genuinely angry. "He did it, I didn't."

"But maybe you have to forgive him, if you want to stay married."

"I haven't figured that out yet."

Pascale nodded, and a few minutes later, they reached

the market. They stayed for two hours buying bread, and cheeses, and fruit and wine, some wonderful terrines, and a strawberry tart that made Pascale's mouth water just looking at it. And when they got back to the house with their purchases, they found Eric and John sprawled out in deck chairs, while John smoked a cigar, and they both looked relaxed and happy. And as the women came in with their string bags and a big basket, John told them that the plumber had come to fix the toilet. But as soon as he had left, the one in Eric and Diana's bathroom had flooded, and Marius was upstairs trying to fix it.

"I don't think we should buy the house," Eric said matter-of-factly.

"There's a news flash," John said, waving his cigar at his wife. "I hope you didn't spend too much money on food."

"Of course not, I only bought cheeses that had gone bad, stale bread, and the fruit that had gone rotten. It was a real bargain."

"Very funny," he said, turning back to Eric and drawing on his cigar.

The foursome ate lunch outside, and afterward they all swam, and Eric took Diana out in the sailboat. She seemed reluctant to go with him at first, but eventually he convinced her. She wasn't a big sailor, and she seemed determined not to open up to him. But Pascale had gone to take a nap by then, and John disappeared shortly after.

And there was nothing else to do, so Diana decided to go with him.

And by the time the Donnallys emerged from their room at six o'clock, Eric and Diana were speaking, and looking far more relaxed than they had that morning. Things were obviously not perfect with them, but they were a little better than they had been.

Pascale cooked squab for them that night, from an old recipe of her mother's, and they ate the strawberry tart she and Diana had bought at the market. It was delicious. They topped it off with *café filtre,* and afterward they sat around the table and chatted. Robert was coming the next day, and Diana asked Pascale if she knew anything more about the mysterious friend he said he might be bringing.

"I haven't heard anything more from him since I left New York. I assume he'll tell us when he gets here, but I really don't think it'll be that actress. They hardly know each other. I think we were worried for nothing." In the relaxed atmosphere of St Tropez, she was feeling less concerned.

"I hope so," Diana said, looking stern. Particularly after Eric's infidelity, she seemed like the guardian of all morals. She had already promised herself she was not going to let Robert make a fool of himself, and if he told them he had invited Gwen Thomas to St Tropez, Diana had every intention of telling him what a mistake he was making, and what an insult to Anne's memory it was for him to be dating some starlet. She was hardly that, at her age, but Diana was quite convinced, as was Pascale, that she couldn't possibly be a decent person, and all they wanted was to protect Robert from himself.

But the next day, when he arrived, Robert looked entirely respectable, as he got out of his rented car with Mandy. She was wearing a white T-shirt and white jeans, a straw hat, and Robert was wearing a blue cotton shirt and khakis. They both looked fresh and clean and wholesome, and very American, and a little startled when they saw the villa.

"This isn't how I remembered it, from the pictures," he said, looking puzzled. "Am I crazy, or is this a little more rustic?"

"A *lot* more rustic," Pascale explained, as John shot her an amused look.

"And wait till you see the maid and the gardener," he added, "but we got half our money back, so it's worth it."

"Why did they do that?" Robert looked surprised by what John had told him.

"Because they screwed us. They're French. What do you expect?" Pascale shot him an evil glance as he said it, but he wasn't daunted. "To be blunt, when Pascale got here, apparently it looked like *The Fall of the House of Usher*. She spent two days cleaning it up, and it's fine, just don't try to flush the toilets, and don't expect to see it in

Architectural Digest." Robert nodded with a look of amusement, and Mandy looked instantly worried.

"Can we use the toilets?" There was a note of panic in her voice that instantly amused Pascale. Anne had always complained to her that her daughter was spoiled and very fussy.

"Sure, you can," John reassured her, "just wear your galoshes."

"Oh my God," she said, as Pascale tried not to laugh. "Should we go to a hotel? Can we stay here?" She had visions of not being able to use the plumbing at all, and would have preferred a hotel.

"We've been here for two days," Diana said practically, "and we're surviving just fine. Why don't I show you your room," but when she did, Mandy was only slightly reassured. The plumbing was gurgling and running, and she noticed a damp, musty smell in the room. She was one of those people who never felt totally comfortable, or at ease, when she left home. "I'll open the windows for you," Diana said, trying to be helpful, and when she tried, one of them literally fell out and into the garden. "I'll have the gardener come and put it back in again," she said with a smile at Mandy's horrified expression. And five minutes later, she went back to her father and asked him if he thought the house was safe. She also had a phobia about spiders and bugs, and the house clearly had more than its fair share.

"I really don't think we should stay here," Mandy said cautiously to her father, and then suggested they look at the Hotel Byblos, the best hotel in St Tropez. One of her friends had stayed there the year before.

"We'll be fine here," he said reassuringly, "it'll be fun. It's more fun to stay here with our friends. We don't need to go to a hotel." And Eric had already told him that the little sailboat was sound, and he was dying to go out in it with him.

"Maybe I should go to Venice early," she said, still looking worried. She was meeting friends there.

"Whatever you decide," he said calmly. Anne had always been much better at handling her than he had. He got impatient with her when she was nervous or worried, and it was obvious that she preferred luxurious to "rustic." But at her age, he didn't think a few days in a crumbling villa would hurt her, bugs and all. And he actually liked it. It was comfortable, and everything was a little frayed around the edges, but he thought the house had charm, and he had already told Pascale he liked it, which pleased her. She was feeling very guilty that it was so much less grand than she had promised. But they had all adjusted fairly well.

The first minor crisis came late that afternoon, when Mandy went to lie on her bed and read for a while. She had just gotten comfortable when it collapsed beneath her. Two of the legs were broken, and it had been carefully propped up to conceal them. The moment she moved, she shifted the delicate balance, and wound up on the floor. She let out a small scream, and Pascale stopped in to ask her what was wrong, and then laughed when she saw her sprawled out on the floor.

"Oh dear, I'll call Marius to come fix it."

But when he appeared to attempt the repair, the bed had been glued back together so often that he couldn't get it to hold this time. And Mandy had to resign herself to sleeping on the mattress flat on the floor, which gave easier access to the spiders and bugs. She was a good sport about it. But Pascale could tell she wasn't pleased, and suspected she'd be leaving for Venice before long.

With his tool kit in hand, Marius left her room in an alcoholic stupor, and she thanked him for his help.

"He's a good guy," John laughed about him later, "and his wife is a real gem. You'll love her outfits," he promised, and when Agathe reappeared late that afternoon, she was wearing a white lace blouse you could see right through over a black bra, and white short shorts that barely covered her bottom. Mandy couldn't help but laugh, although her father looked somewhat shocked.

"I think she's kind of cute," John said, looking amused, and Robert grinned in spite of himself. "Wait till you see her little leopard number, or the hot pink bicycle shorts." Robert chuckled as Mandy disappeared. He'd had fun in the sailboat that afternoon, and he was amused by the decrepit state of the house. To him, it seemed like an adventure, and he was convinced that Anne would have loved it too, and seen the funny side of it. She had always been more adventuresome than her daughter, and wasn't afraid of bugs. Mandy was a city girl.

As Pascale cooked dinner that night, and checked on the chickens she was roasting, the oven door fell off and landed at her feet on the kitchen floor. But Eric managed to repair it. He used baling wire, and created an ingenious system to reattach it, as the others applauded his ingenuity. Although afterward, Mandy mentioned the Byblos to her father again, with a hopeful look. She clearly wasn't enjoying the rustic charm of the house as much as her father and his friends.

"I like it here," her father said simply, "and so do the others." Although, admittedly, it wasn't as much fun for her. There was no one her age for her to hang out with, and she was beginning to think it had been a mistake to come. But she didn't want to hurt anyone's feelings by leaving sooner than planned.

It was her father who finally offered to let her off the hook.

"This isn't much fun for you, sweetheart. The house isn't as comfortable as I thought." And even the little sailboat didn't offer her much distraction. Although her brothers were avid sailors, Mandy had always hated to sail. She loved waterskiing, and going dancing at night, and being with people her own age.

"I love being here with you, Dad," she said honestly. And she had always liked her parents' friends. But it also made her lonely for her mother not seeing her in their midst, although she was fond of Diana and Pascale.

"Do you want to leave earlier for Venice? My feelings won't be hurt." He was happy with the Morrisons and Donnallys, but Mandy felt guilty abandoning him.

"Of course not. I love it here." They both knew it was a stretch of the truth.

"I think you should try to meet up sooner with your friends." And he urged her to go shopping in St Tropez that afternoon, where she ran into a friend staying nearby, in Ramatuelle. He was a very pleasant young man and came by to take her to dinner that night.

The others were going to Le Chabichou for dinner, which Agathe had suggested to them. They left the house in two cars and were in high spirits, except for Eric and Diana, who split up and went in separate cars. Eric seemed subdued, and Diana was far quieter than usual. But they were all pleased with the restaurant, and even more so when they tasted the food. It was superb.

And at eleven o'clock, they were still there, happy and sated, and they had drunk three bottles of wine among them. Even Eric and Diana's spirits had improved, although they weren't sitting next to each other and hadn't spoken to each other all night. Pascale was deep in conversation with Robert, when he mentioned again that he had a friend arriving on Monday. Mandy was supposed to leave by the weekend, if not before.

"Is it anyone we know?" Pascale asked casually, dying of curiosity, but not wanting to sound as though she was prying into his affairs.

"I don't think so. It's a friend I met two months ago, when I was out with Mandy." Pascale pricked up her ears then, wondering if it was the infamous actress, or at least she assumed she was infamous and Diana agreed. "I'm sure you've heard of her," he continued, "she's a very nice woman. She's staying with friends in Antibes this week, and I thought it might be fun for you all to meet her."

"Is this"—Pascale struggled for the right words, torn between curiosity and good manners—"someone you're interested in, Robert?"

"We're just friends," he said simply, and then realized that everyone was listening, and he looked faintly embarrassed. "She's an actress. Gwen Thomas. She won an Oscar last year." Diana stared across the table at him, in open disapproval, the moment he said it. She was more critical of everything these days.

"Why would she want to come here?" she said bluntly. "We're not very interesting, and the house is a mess. Do you really want her to come here?" They were all praying that he didn't, they didn't want a stranger in their midst, particularly one who was more than likely to be difficult and spoiled. And the two women were certain that "the actress," as they referred to her among themselves, was trying to take advantage of him in some way. They loved him dearly, and after so many years sheltered in marriage, they assumed he was naïve.

"She's a very nice person. I think you'll all like her," Robert said calmly, as the men nodded, curious to meet her, and the two women frowned.

"This isn't exactly Rodeo Drive," Diana persisted, trying to discourage him, but he looked unimpressed either by her lack of enthusiasm for meeting Gwen, or by Pascale's. John and Eric were actually secretly intrigued, but wouldn't have said it to their wives.

Pascale couldn't think of anything worse than having to entertain some spoiled prima donna. She was certain Gwen Thomas would surely be a nightmare, she was famous enough to be. It would ruin their whole vacation. And possibly Robert's life. "How long is she staying?"

"A few days, a week at most. It depends on when she has to get back to L.A. She's going into rehearsal for a movie, and she wanted to rest first. I thought this might be fun for her." He said it in a fatherly, protective way. "I think Anne would have liked her. They share a lot of the same views and attitudes. She likes the same books and music and plays." Pascale looked at John with worried eyes, and Diana even glanced at Eric. Neither woman believed for a minute that they were just "friends." They were sure that Gwen Thomas was out to get him, and that he was an innocent about to be slaughtered. It was inconceivable to either woman that the actress's motives were pure.

And as silence fell on all of them, Eric asked for the check, and they each paid their share, while John pored over the bill, determined to find a mistake. He always assumed that restaurants were out to cheat him, which was why Pascale hated going out to dinner with him. By the time he finished pulling the check apart and recalculating everything, he always spoiled her dinner. But she was so unnerved by the impending arrival of Robert's "friend" that she paid no attention to John. She could hardly wait to discuss it all with Diana the next day, and she thought it a bold move for Robert to bring Gwen here. It seemed too soon after Anne's death to be dating anyone. The match and the visit seemed wrong to her in every way.

"Shall we go then?" Robert asked pleasantly, as they went back to the cars, and drove back to the house. Pascale and Diana rode with John on the way back and they talked animatedly about their plans to "save" Robert from the evil Gwen.

"Why don't you give the girl a chance and see how she behaves?" John said sensibly, and both women were outraged. It made him wonder if they were jealous of Gwen, but he wouldn't have dared suggest it to them. All they said was that they were worried about Robert, and owed it to Anne to protect him from a girl who was clearly unworthy of him, according to them.

They all said good night to each other at the house, and Mandy was already home in bed. But Pascale lay in bed thinking about the nightmare that was about to descend on them, and turned to John with a worried look.

"What about the paparazzi?" she asked anxiously.

"What about them?" he asked blankly. He had no idea what she was thinking. Her imagination seemed to be running wild.

"They'll be all over us if that woman comes here. We won't have another peaceful minute for the rest of the vacation." It was a valid thought, and something none of them had considered yet.

"I don't think there's much we can do on that score. I'm sure she's used to it, and can handle it," he said, sounding unconcerned. "I must admit, I'm surprised he asked her here, particularly with you and Diana down his throat," he said, looking amused.

"We're not down his throat," she fumed, looking very French. "We care about him. She probably won't stay more than a day, when she sees the house," Pascale said hopefully. "Maybe she'll leave, when she realizes we're on to her. Robert may be an innocent, but the rest of us aren't." And then suddenly John laughed as he listened to her.

"Poor Robert. He should only know what you have in store for him when she gets here. I don't suppose we'll ever get used to the idea of someone else in his life," John said pensively. "Anyone but Anne seems like such an intrusion. But he has a right to do what he wants. He's a grown man, and he needs female companionship. He can't stay alone forever. And if he likes this girl, Pascale, why not? She's beautiful, she's young. He enjoys her company. He could do a lot worse." It actually sounded pretty great to him, more so than he would have admitted to Pascale.

"Are you crazy? What have you been drinking? Don't you know what she is? She's some little tart of an actress, and we have to save him from her." It was an extreme point of view, to say the least. She sounded like Joan of Arc on a crusade.

"I know what you think. But I was just wondering if we have a right to interfere. Maybe he knows what he's doing. And maybe they really only are just friends, and if it's more than that, maybe he's in love with her. Poor Robert. I feel sorry for him." But how sorry could one feel? One of the biggest stars in Hollywood was coming to visit him. If nothing else, it was certainly more exciting than his life had been with Anne.

"I feel sorry for him too. He's an innocent. Which is exactly why we have to protect him. And Mandy would be horrified if she knew about this."

"I don't think you should tell her," John said seriously. "It's up to Robert what he tells his daughter about this woman."

"She'll find out eventually anyway," Pascale said ominously.

"Let him have a little fun after all the sadness he's had over losing Anne. That's probably all this is anyway. Just a good time. We'll find someone decent for him eventually," she said firmly.

"He's not exactly doing badly on his own," John reminded her. "Hell, she's a knockout, and one of the most well-known actresses in the country."

"Precisely," Pascale said as though he had proven the point to her. "And *that* is why we have to protect him. She can't possibly be a good person, given all that," Pascale said emphatically.

"Poor Robert," John said again with a smile. And as he drifted off to sleep that night, snuggled up to Pascale, John knew he should feel sorry for him, but in spite of all of Pascale's dire predictions, it sounded pretty good to him.

8

THE REST OF THE WEEK rolled by, with them all eating dinner at home, and in restaurants, relaxing and lying in the sun, swimming, and sailing. And Mandy left on Saturday, only a day earlier than planned. In spite of everything, she and her father had had a great time. He had told her vaguely that there was a friend visiting him the following week, and she was relieved that he would be surrounded by friends. She kept meaning to ask him who it was, but in the flurry of activity before she left, she forgot. She assumed it was one of his old friends, or someone from the bench, and it never occurred to her that it might be a woman and not a man.

On Sunday night, as Pascale and Diana cooked dinner, there was a sense of anticipation over Gwen's arrival the next day. Robert hadn't said much more about her, but it was obvious even when he mentioned her, that he was excited to be seeing Gwen. Pascale and Diana, and even

Eric and John to some extent, were still curious and suspicious of her. In spite of all their preconceived notions, they weren't sure what to expect.

Robert seemed like a babe in the woods to them. He hadn't dated in years, and certainly never anyone like this woman. Her world was completely unfamiliar to him. She was famous and sophisticated, and she led a life they all disapproved of, on principle. She wasn't "respectable," as Pascale said, she was divorced, and she had never had children, which suggested, to them at least, a certain selfishness and egocentricity. She was obviously wrapped up in herself and her career. Pascale hadn't been able to have children. They were sure that Gwen Thomas hated children. They found a thousand reasons to dislike her, even before they laid eyes on her.

When Monday morning came, Gwen called, and when Robert talked to her, she said she would arrive by car at lunchtime. They were sure she would drive up in a long black limousine, probably with a liveried chauffeur, or something equally absurd. They had had Marius fix her bed, in what had been Mandy's room, but none of them would have minded if it broke again. They were like kids at camp, or in boarding school, waiting to torture the new girl.

Robert was aware of none of it as he showered and dressed before she arrived. He was wearing white shorts, a white sport shirt, and a pair of brown sandals, and he looked very handsome. He was a good-looking man, and with a tan he looked better than ever, younger and healthier than he had in months, or even years.

Pascale suggested they not wait lunch for her. But Robert said he would skip lunch too, and take her out to a bistro in St Tropez if she was hungry. It seemed more polite to him than simply ignoring her, and eating with the others. But he urged them all to go on and eat without him. He was as calm and pleasant as ever, with no idea how resentful they were of Gwen. Had he suspected what was in store for her, he would never have asked her to come.

Pascale was organizing lunch for them at noon, when she heard a car drive up, and glanced out the kitchen window. But all she saw was a tiny Deux Chevaux, and then she saw a pretty redheaded woman climb out of it wearing a denim miniskirt, a white T-shirt, and a pair of flat white sandals. She looked very plain, but at the same time very fresh and wholesome and clean. She was wearing her hair in a braid, and it struck Pascale for an instant that she looked a little like Mandy, only prettier. She wondered who the woman was at first, and then realized with a start that it was Gwen. There was no limousine in sight, no driver, no paparazzi, and Gwen looked around as she carried a large straw tote bag, and a single small suitcase.

In spite of herself, Pascale asked Marius to go out and help her. And as she saw him go, she spotted Robert leaving the house. He must have been watching for her from an upstairs window, like a boy waiting for a friend to come.

The minute Gwen saw Robert, she beamed, and even Pascale had to admit that her smile was dazzling, her skin beautiful, and she had spectacular legs in the miniskirt and sandals. She had an extraordinarily good figure. And she looked happy and at ease with him, as they headed slowly toward the kitchen. And within another instant, Pascale was staring at her, as Robert introduced her, and smiled proudly at Gwen.

"It's very nice to meet you," Pascale lied. "We've heard a lot about you."

"I've heard a lot about you too," Gwen said pleasantly. "You must be Pascale. How has the house been?" She shook Pascale's hand, and seemed not to be aware of the chilly reception she was getting. She was easygoing, and unaffected, and surprisingly unpretentious. She had offered to carry her bag upstairs herself, but Robert had Marius do it, and then Gwen offered to help Pascale with lunch, and she stepped right up to the sink. She washed her hands, and seemed to expect to work with Pascale.

"I—no . . . ahh . . . it's fine. You don't need to help me." So instead Gwen hung out in the kitchen with Pascale and

Robert. He was talking to her animatedly about all the work Pascale had done in the house, and how comfortable she had made it for all of them.

"They should pay us to stay here," Robert said admiringly, as John walked into the kitchen.

"Now that's an idea I'll second," John said, glancing at her, wondering who she was. And whoever she was, she was incredibly pretty, he thought to himself, and when he saw his wife's face, he realized who he was talking to. He hadn't recognized Gwen at first, and what surprised him most was that he didn't expect her to look so human, so lovely, or so young. She certainly didn't look her forty-one years, but Pascale wondered if it was natural, or if she had had "work done." She was wearing very little makeup, and seemed surprisingly natural in every way. She had simple, unassuming ways, a natural kindness and warmth, and staggering good looks. And as John looked Gwen over carefully, it was impossible to see in her the devil Pascale had described. And soon Pascale looked surprised and ill at ease in the face of Gwen's obvious charm.

Ten minutes later, their lunch was on the table, and the Morrisons appeared, and they stopped dead in their tracks at their first glimpse of her. She wasn't at all what they had imagined. She was far more beautiful and natural, and as she spoke to them, seemed genuinely warm.

But even in the face of that, Diana told herself Gwen was an actress and could fool anyone.

Sensing none of their malevolent thoughts about her, Gwen sat down at the table with them, after carrying several platters to the table. She had jumped right in, helping Pascale, without hesitation or restraint. Robert had offered to take her to a restaurant for lunch, but she said she'd be happier here, having lunch with his friends. She said that Robert had talked so much about them that she was happy to meet them at last. And as she said it, Pascale and Diana exchanged an evil look. They remained convinced that beneath the appealing exterior lurked a bitch.

As they sat down to lunch, Robert asked Gwen comfortably about Antibes. He seemed very much at ease with her, and she said she had had fun, and done a lot of reading, and lying in the sun. She'd been exhausted when she arrived.

"What did you read?" he asked with interest, as the others sat watching her, feeling fascinated and awkward. There was a quality of unreality to sitting there chatting with her, after seeing her so often on screen. Gwen told Robert, in answer to his question, that she had read a number of very good new novels, and named them all. They were all the same books Pascale and Diana had just read.

"I'm always hoping to get a film out of things I read. But it's not easy to find new properties. Most of the scripts are so flat and so boring," she said by way of explanation. She said she had performed in a movie based on a Grisham novel recently, and really enjoyed doing it. And neither Pascale nor Diana admitted to being impressed, but were nonetheless.

Robert had read two of the four books she'd read, and he had to agree with her. He liked them. And they talked animatedly about that, and assorted other things, until Pascale served coffee. Eric and John had entered the conversation by then, but the girls were holding out. They didn't want to be seduced by her, although it was clear that the men were rapidly being swayed by her charm. It was easy to see why Robert liked being with her. She was easygoing, intelligent, had a nice sense of humor, and was easy to be around. Far easier at this point than Diana or Pascale. It was Gwen who made small talk with all of them, asking about what they had been doing during their vacation, and carrying the conversational ball, although neither Pascale nor Diana made it easy for her. They answered her in monosyllables and occasionally didn't answer her at all, although she didn't seem to notice or mind.

And then, as the meal drew to a close, Agathe wandered in, adding a little comic relief for all concerned. Agathe seemed oblivious to the effect she caused, as she hummed to herself, carrying a stack of towels in front of her, with one of her poodles prancing behind her. She left the kitchen almost as quickly as she had entered it. Gwen stared after her, as Agathe's generous behind waddled past in rhythm to the music. She was wearing leopard print shorts, and a rhine-stone bra, with her favorite red satin high heels.

"What was that?" Gwen whispered to Robert after Agathe had left. "She looked like Liberace in drag."

And in spite of themselves, the others laughed.

"*That* is Agathe," Robert answered with a grin, amused by Gwen's apt description of her. One of the things he liked about Gwen was that she made him laugh more than he had in a long time. "She's the housekeeper," Robert said happily. "She usually wears a black uniform and a lace apron, but she dressed especially for you to-day," he teased, as his friends saw the look on his face. He seemed so at ease with her, he was usually so serious, sometimes even somber, and he was more lighthearted than they'd ever seen. Pascale thought he was making a fool of himself, while Diana wondered if the color of Gwen's hair was natural. It was a striking shade of red, but could have been real, and in fact, was. She was a natural redhead, rarest of all birds in Hollywood, with huge chestnut eyes, perfect skin, and no freckles. There was a lot to hate about her, if one were so inclined.

"Can she actually clean?" Gwen was still inquiring about Agathe as Robert shook his head, he was vastly amused by her, and in surprisingly good humor. He had been during the whole vacation, and Pascale couldn't help wondering if it was in anticipation of Gwen's visit. He certainly didn't look as grief-stricken as he had months before, but John had already said that it wasn't fair to measure Robert's grief by his efforts to be pleasant and not burden them with his sorrow.

"Pascale says she's a pretty hard worker," Robert said about their maid with the unusual costumes and the flock of dogs that never stopped barking. "You already met her husband. He drinks a bit, but he's nice enough. They came with the house," he said by way of explanation, as Gwen laughed.

"What's everyone doing this afternoon?" Diana inquired, looking pointedly at them. She had already decided that if they said they were taking "naps," she was going to stand in the hallway between their rooms and busy herself. She was prepared to do anything she had to, to protect Robert's virtue, and the least she could do, she felt, was make things difficult for them. She felt she owed that much to Anne.

"I wouldn't mind going into St Tropez for a little while, if no one minds, to do a little shopping." Gwen had told Robert in an earlier conversation that she loved to shop, and seldom had the time.

"I'll come with you," he said quickly, as the others stared. It was an open secret in the group that he hated to shop. And so had Anne. He was suddenly a different man.

"Do you like to sail?" Pascale asked, hoping to show her up.

"I love to sail," Gwen said quietly, and then turned to Robert. "Would you rather do that?" She looked at Robert gently as she asked.

"We can do both," he said sensibly. "Why don't we go to St Tropez first."

"I'll get my handbag," Gwen said, and disappeared to her room to get it, as Robert smiled at his friends. He had no concept of the jealousy that lurked in Pascale and Diana's hearts. They were behaving like their own evil twins.

"She's a nice woman, isn't she?" he said, happy to share her with them.

"Yes," Pascale said through clenched teeth, as her husband shot her a quelling look. He thought she and Diana had gone far enough, and Robert and Gwen were both being good sports. And if asked, Eric would have agreed with him. Fortunately, Robert seemed not to notice how subtly hostile the two women had been. He admired Gwen so much, it was hard for him to imagine that anyone would be less than dazzled by her. Although at least two of his best friends were determined to resist, unbeknownst to him. They saw her as a siren and a threat, to be chased off at all costs. No matter what it took. For his own good, of course.

Robert followed Gwen out of the house, after saying good-bye to them, and a few minutes later, they heard the Deux Chevaux drive off, as the two men looked at their wives disapprovingly.

"What do you say you two lighten up when they get back? She seems like a nice woman, and she's Robert's guest." Eric said it as much to Pascale as to his wife, and it was obvious that John agreed with him as he nodded his head.

"She certainly got your number quickly, didn't she?" Diana said bitterly, alluding to his recent wanderings. "I didn't realize redheads were your type. But then again, I guess there's a lot about you I don't know these days." It was a blow below the belt, and he didn't look pleased, but he held his ground.

"That's not what we're talking about. If I were Gwen, I wouldn't bother to unpack, and I'd go straight to the nearest hotel, instead of taking a lot of guff from us. She doesn't have to be here. Robert wants her to be. She's doing it for him. She obviously cares about him, and it's not her fault he has four friends who were attached to Anne, and can't get over it. It's up to Robert who he wants in his life, not up to us to screw it up for him." What he said made sense, whether they admitted it or not.

"She's an actress," Pascale added angrily. "She can convince anyone of anything, you, John, Robert . . . that's what she does. He doesn't even know who she is."

"Maybe he knows better than we do, Pascale. He's not a fool. He's a grown man, he's intelligent. She's a beautiful woman, and she's a good sport if she's willing to put up with us. I wouldn't, in her shoes. I'd have told us all to go screw ourselves, and walked out halfway through lunch. You two hardly said a word. I'm sure there are plenty of people who would knock themselves out to be with her, and be nice to her. She doesn't need us to give her a hard time. What do you say we lighten up when they get back from town?" He was trying to appeal to both of them. He had never seen either woman act this way. And John seconded it.

"Eric's right. We're hurting Robert as much as we are her, if we give her a hard time. Why don't we just let him figure it out for himself?" Besides, he didn't want to admit it to Pascale in so many words, but he liked Gwen, far more than he thought he would. And he liked the way she treated his friends, with kindness and respect, and humor, and courtesy. There was something incredibly decent and sensitive about her, and John was as embarrassed as Eric by how his wife had behaved.

"What's wrong with you two?" Diana interjected again. "Just because she has good legs and wears a miniskirt, you two are suddenly in love with her. She's twenty-two years younger than Robert, and he's making a fool of himself. And just how long do you think it's going to last? Some handsome young actor will come along, and she'll dump Robert on his ear, and he'll be heartbroken if he falls for her."

"Maybe he already has—and maybe she's fallen for him. Why not let him work it out for himself? And what's wrong, even if it doesn't last, if he has some fun along the way? It might be a great story to tell his grandchildren one day, about the affair he had with a beautiful young actress one summer. Worse things happen. A lot worse," Eric said, glancing at his wife. "He's single, for heaven's sake. He doesn't owe anyone any explanations and certainly not us. What right do we have to stand in his way?"

"Do all men think with only one part of their anatomy?" Diana said to her husband pointedly. "I get it. She's beautiful. I'll concede that much. But none of us knows who the hell she is, and I'll bet Robert doesn't either. I just don't want to see him do something stupid, or get hurt, or have some Hollywood bimbo take advantage of him."

"How?" Eric persisted in the argument. "What's she going to get from him? She probably makes more money than any of us. She's not going to get anywhere by sleeping with him. He can't give her a part in a movie. He can't even fix her parking tickets, for chrissake. And if it weren't for him, she'd probably be staying in some four-star hotel, and not sleeping on a bed that will probably collapse in the middle of the night, with a toilet that won't flush, a maid who'll blow smoke in her face, and four people making her miserable, in the guise of defending a man who wants to be with her anyway, and maybe should. Just what exactly do you think she's getting out of this?" What he said made sense, although neither woman was yet ready to concede, but he had a point, as John nodded his head and agreed.

"What if he marries her?" Pascale asked angrily. "Then what?"

"Why don't we worry about it then?" John intervened, and Eric laughed suddenly.

"I remember the first time we all had dinner with you, Pascale. You hardly spoke English, you were an hour late, you wore a black satin dress that was so tight you couldn't breathe, and you were a ballerina, which isn't so different from being an actress after all, in some people's eyes at least. And Anne and Diana were suspicious of you too. They got over it. They fell in love with you. . . . Everyone gave you a chance. Why can't you do that for her?" There was silence in the room as he looked at her, and then finally Pascale turned away and shook her head. But he had scored a hit, and she knew it. She had been a frightened, nervous, starving ballerina when John fell in love with her, and they could have accused her of all the same things. What complicated it all now was how much they had loved Anne. But Anne was gone. And Gwen was the woman Robert wanted to be with. He had trusted them, in a sense, by bringing her here, and they were violating that trust by being unkind to her. Pascale could see Eric's point, although she wasn't ready to admit it in so many words.

And Diana conceded nothing as she put their lunch dishes in the sink. She was still so angry at Eric, she didn't want to hear anything he said. Gwen was just another pretty face and a pair of good legs he wanted to chase after, as far as she was concerned. And the fact that John agreed with him meant nothing to her. She was so angry at everyone these days, Gwen was just another place to vent the anguish she felt.

The men went out to the garden to smoke cigars after that, and Pascale hung around the kitchen to help Diana, and after a long silence, she looked at her friend with a questioning glance.

"What do you think?" Pascale asked with a worried frown.

"It's too soon to know what she's really like," Diana said stubbornly, and Pascale nodded agreement, but in her heart of hearts, she was no longer quite as convinced. Eric had made some good points.

And in the car, on the way into St Tropez, Gwen was questioning Robert about his friends.

"Are you sure your friends don't mind my intruding on you, Robert? I feel like an interloper barging in. You're all used to being together, after all these years, and suddenly there I am, larger than life. It's a big adjustment for them." She had sensed their discomfort during lunch, more than he had in fact. He just told himself they were shy because of who she was, and he said as much to her, which made her smile at him. She knew, just as Diana and Pascale did, that he was naïve, and she loved that about him. He had a way of only seeing the good at times, and simplifying things. "I think this is harder for them than you realize. Seeing you with someone else is a big change for all of them."

"It's a big change for me too," he said, looking serious for a moment, and thinking of Anne. But he didn't want to let himself slip into sadness about her. No matter how grief-stricken he was, and had been, it wouldn't bring her back. "But we all have to adjust." He looked at her sympathetically then. "I just don't want it to be hard on you. Were they rude to you?" he asked, looking worried, wondering if he had missed something.

"Of course not. I just feel a certain reserve and resistance. I expected it. I'm fine with it. I just don't want to make things awkward for you with your friends."

"They're like my family, Gwen. We've shared a lot of history, and a lot of years. I'd really like them to get to know you, and to appreciate you, as I do." He knew that they couldn't possibly resist. Or so he thought. She wasn't as sure.

"I think you need to give them time, Robert," she said sensibly, as they approached the heart of St Tropez, and he looked for a place to park. "It may take them longer than you think." If they even gave her a chance. She was well aware that they might never open their hearts or doors to her. She wasn't as sure as Robert that they'd adjust and welcome her in.

"You don't know my friends. Trust me, Gwen. They're

going to be in love with you by the end of dinner tonight. What's not to love?" he said, smiling at her.

"I'm not Anne," she said gently. "That's the first strike against me, in their eyes. And I'm famous . . . I'm an actress . . . I'm from Hollywood . . . I'm sure they think I'm weird. Particularly, if they read the tabloids. It's a lot for people to swallow at first. Believe me, I've been there. Those are the things that make people hate you till they know you, if they ever do. I'm guilty until proven innocent, not the reverse."

"Not in my house, and not with my friends," he said confidently, as she smiled knowingly at him, and leaned over to kiss his cheek. She wasn't going to force it down his throat, but she had sensed their resistance at lunch, and it was a phenomenon that was familiar to her. It hurt sometimes, and was disappointing, but it was something she'd been through again and again, and they had thirty years of history with him. That was a tough mystique to break. And she wasn't going to force herself on them. She was too smart for that. She was just going to go about her business quietly, and hope that in time they would let her in. But above all, she was determined not to push. And it was too soon to know what was going to happen with Robert anyway.

He found a parking space finally, turned to her in the tiny car and put an arm around her, and gave her a gentle kiss. "Well, shall we hit the shops, Miss Thomas?"

"Sounds good to me, your honor." She smiled lovingly at him. She was glad she had come to visit him, even if his friends were visibly less than pleased.

"Do you think everyone will recognize you?"

"Probably. Can you live with that?" she asked him, looking faintly worried. It could be overwhelming at times, particularly if you weren't used to it. And celebrity was a world Robert knew nothing about. She liked that about him too. Being with him always felt right and was real.

"I guess I'd better get used to it, if you're going to be spending time with me." He always felt lucky to be with her, not because of her fame, but because of who she was, as a human being, not as a star. "Let's go," he said, as they hopped out of the car, and they hadn't gone ten steps before someone stopped them and asked for her autograph. He smiled as she paused and signed a piece of paper, and then again two minutes later when two young men asked her to pose for a photograph. She handled it graciously, and moved on quickly, doing her best not to let it interfere with Robert too much. But it was what it was, and they managed to enjoy the shops anyway, and stopped in a sidewalk café afterward for a glass of wine. And as usual, they had a terrific time, just talking and laughing and being together. They never ran out of things to talk about, and always had fun.

They chatted about a wide variety of topics, his work, her films, their ideals, their parents, his children, and her childhood. He knew she had wanted to be a teacher, and never once suspected, early on, that she would become an actress, let alone win an Oscar. She had told him what that had been like, and what it had meant to her, and how hard it was now to select roles that would be equally meaningful to her.

"Sometimes you just have to do something fun that you love. Every picture can't win you an Oscar," she said matter-of-factly, and then she told him more about the one she was about to start, and the actors who had been hired to work with her. It was a murder mystery, and her costar was even more famous than she, which reminded her of something else she'd meant to tell him. "I have a couple of friends in the area. They're on a yacht, and she's a beauty. It's called the *Talitha G,* and belongs to Paul Getty." Robert had heard of it, but never seen it. It was a classic motor yacht, with an extraordinarily elegant interior. It was all marble and antiques, and her friends had it for two weeks. She was wondering if Robert would like his friends to visit them on the yacht. "I didn't want to extend an invitation to them until I asked how you felt about it."

"It sounds exciting," he said honestly. "I've always wanted to see it. I read an article about it in a magazine years ago, and showed it to Anne. She was more of a sailboat aficionado, but she thought it sounded terrific. It looked beautiful in the photographs."

"It is. I saw it last year, and thought about chartering it, but it seemed a little showy for just me, and a bunch of other folks from L.A." He was impressed that she'd even thought about it.

"I think the others would love to see it," he said warmly, and then she told him who her friends were who had chartered it, and he laughed. "The ladies in the group are going to faint when you tell them that," Robert said with a look of amusement. Gwen's life was entirely different from his. She was part of a world that was so foreign to all of them. She knew people, and bandied names whom most people had only read about or dreamed of. The actor who had rented the *Talitha G* was a star of major proportions, Henry Adams, and his wife was a well-known supermodel. And they had on the boat, as their guests, two other actors who were major stars.

"They're all old friends and nice people," Gwen said with a smile. "Maybe your friends would like to meet them."

"They're not going to be able to resist an opportunity like this," he said with a broad grin.

"I'll call them on the boat when we get back. They were all at the Hôtel du Cap last week," she said, smiling. "It's rough work, but someone has to do it."

"Do you suppose they'll mind coming to the villa?"

"Of course not, they'll love it." She had worked with

each of them on movies in the past five years, and it brought into focus for Robert again how important her career was, and how far she had come with it. The only thing that surprised him was how without artifice she was, how unassuming, and how real.

And when they got back to the house, he took her sailing. She wasn't quite as adept at it as Anne, but she was a good sport, and didn't complain when they took a sharp turn and she fell in. She was laughing when he pulled her back into the boat, and he turned away when she nearly lost the top of her bikini. He didn't want to embarrass her, but he was more than a little impressed by her spectacular figure. It was hard not to be. They spent the rest of the afternoon in the boat, and when they got back, Pascale and Diana were already cooking dinner, and barely said hello when they walked through.

"Would you prefer to go out?" he asked Gwen discreetly. Her hair was wet, and she was wrapped in a big beach towel, and carrying her sandals, as they walked into the house in bare feet.

"No, I'd love to stay here. We can go out some other time. I'll call Henry. Maybe we can have dinner on the boat tomorrow night, if that appeals to everyone. He says the food is delicious. They have a great chef."

"I don't think they'd care if they had to eat dog food, just so they could be on it, and see them," he said in a whisper as they checked the pantry for a snack and settled for a handful of nuts. He offered her something to drink, and she helped herself to some mineral water.

"I'll come back and help in a few minutes," she promised as Pascale and Diana walked back into the kitchen, and Pascale insisted rather grimly that there was no need to. And as she did, Robert realized that Gwen was right. He had never seen Pascale or Diana behave that way before. There was something cold and almost hostile about both women, which distressed him on behalf of Gwen.

Robert and Gwen disappeared upstairs, and Gwen went into her bedroom to dress, and the moment she sat on the bed, it collapsed again, and she laughed out loud. It was a perfect scene.

She knocked on Robert's door a minute later, and he appeared in a towel. He had been just about to get into the shower. "I think they booby-trapped my bed," she whispered, and he smiled at her.

"No, it did that last week too. I'll get Marius to fix it. I'm sorry, Gwen," he said with genuine remorse. He wanted her to have a good time, and he was afraid that she wouldn't. But she seemed more amused than annoyed. Nothing seemed to bother Gwen, not even the others' cool reception of her. She realized that it was based on concern for their friend, rather than anything more malicious, which made it a little easier for her.

Robert went downstairs to find Marius, and Gwen went

to shower, and when she emerged in a pink terrycloth robe she had bought at the Ritz, the bed was repaired, and Robert had disappeared to take his own shower. They met in the hallway, coincidentally twenty minutes later, on their way downstairs. She was wearing pale yellow silk pants, and a matching sleeveless silk sweater, with a flowered shawl over one arm, and gold sandals. And she was wearing a minimum of makeup. She looked not so much a movie star as a very beautiful woman.

"You look lovely," he said honestly, and he couldn't help but notice her perfume. It was light and flowery and very sexy. And for the fraction of an instant, his heart ached for Anne, but he tried to tell himself that one thing had nothing to do with the other. It was just that he missed her, and no matter how spectacular Gwen was, she wasn't Anne. But she was still a very fine person, and he enjoyed being with her. Reminding himself of it helped as he followed her down the stairs and back to the kitchen. Eric was there, drinking some wine and talking to Pascale, and Diana had gone upstairs to dress for dinner. John was outside, smoking a cigar and taking pictures of the sunset. The house sat at the same angle as the cafés in town, which allowed them to see the sunset, which was rare in St Tropez.

"What can I do to help?" Gwen offered easily, as Robert poured them both wine, and he handed her glass to her, and Pascale's whole demeanor seemed to tense. She was in a tough spot now, because if she warmed up to Gwen, Diana would feel betrayed.

"You can't do anything," she said bluntly. And then to soften the blow of the way she'd said it to Gwen, Robert told Pascale of the treat Gwen had in store for them the next day. He said friends of hers were coming over with a fabulous yacht, and they might even be able to have dinner on it. "I hate boats," Pascale said, putting some potatoes into the oven with the roast. The way she said it suddenly told Robert Gwen had been right about his friends.

"You'll like this one," Robert assured her, and told her all about it. Eric looked intrigued as he listened, and then John walked into the room, halfway through the conversation, and looked admiringly at Gwen with a smile. And she smiled back. The exchange did not escape Pascale.

"What boat?" John asked, looking blank, as he set his camera down on the table, and accepted a glass of wine from Eric. "Are we chartering a boat? We already have one." The one they had was so insignificant, it made them all laugh. "We don't need to spend any more money," John said firmly, pretending to growl. He still couldn't take his eyes off Gwen.

"I thought we'd buy one," Robert said expansively, and he could almost see John pale beneath his tan.

"Here? In France? Why? Are you crazy?" And then suddenly he realized Robert was teasing. "All right, all right, I get it. So what boat is it?" Robert told him, and as Diana walked into the room, wearing white slacks and a colorful blouse, he told them all who would be on it, and who was coming to visit the next day, thanks to Gwen.

"You're kidding, right?" Diana asked, looking half annoyed, half intrigued. It was certainly an interesting turn of events.

"No, I'm not," Robert said proudly. There were some aspects of Gwen's life that actually amused him. Being able to introduce his friends to three major movie stars and a supermodel was definitely one of them. Although there were other things he liked even better about her. But this was fun.

He looked gratefully at Gwen, who had called the Adamses before she got dressed, and arranged for them to be at the villa by lunchtime tomorrow. They were all going to motor around for the afternoon, and maybe stop to swim somewhere, and then they would anchor off the villa for dinner. For once, even Diana and Pascale were somewhat speechless. It was hard to complain about an invitation like that. And for a while, they all broke into animated conversation, although they failed to include Gwen in it, or to thank her for what she had done for them. But Robert did later, when they took a walk in the garden after dinner. The others hadn't been particularly nice to her, although Eric and John had made an effort. But Pascale and Diana were still holding out. John actually spent considerable time talking to her, despite the fact that Pascale was glaring at him. But by the time coffee was served, there was no question in John's mind, he liked her, she appreciated the effort he had made to talk to her, and she was grateful to him. Of all of them, with the exception of Robert, he had been the nicest to her. And Eric had asked her a number of questions about her work, which only made Diana withdraw more.

It was a relief to get some air after dinner, and Gwen sank happily into one of the garden chairs Pascale had had repainted.

"I'm sorry they're still giving you a tough time. I guess you were right this afternoon," Robert conceded. He had no idea what to do about it, but it was still the first day, and he was hoping for better from them once they all adjusted to her. The women's vendetta against her seemed ridiculous to him, and he didn't fully understand it, but Gwen did. She was used to it. Other people's jealousy, for her looks and success, was a way of life to her. And all Robert wanted was to make it easier for her.

"It'll get better eventually," Gwen said matter-of-factly, "and the boat tomorrow will distract them," she said, as they sat alone together outside. It was like dealing with children. To win them over, you had to keep them busy and amused.

"I never expected this," Robert said unhappily. "I just don't understand what they think they're doing, or why. What's the point of being rude to you?" He was upset about Diana and Pascale's behavior to her. Even he couldn't ignore it anymore.

"They're protecting you," she said philosophically. "They have a lot of preconceived ideas about who and what I am. They'll get over it. I don't want anything from you."

"Can they really be that foolish?" Robert asked once again, looking startled, and she nodded. "But why? You couldn't be nicer to them."

"That has nothing to do with it, and you know it. They're honoring Anne's memory in the only way they know how, and they think they're safeguarding your future. For all they know, I'm some Hollywood monster, Robert. Think about it."

"I hope they grow up soon," he said, sounding annoyed. And then he had an idea, and proposed it to her. "Would you like to go dancing?"

She thought about it for a minute, and then smiled at him, and nodded. "I'd love that. Do you think they'd like to come?"

"I'm not going to invite them," he said bluntly, feeling defiant, and tired of them. "You deserve a little fun without people picking on you."

"I just don't want to hurt anyone's feelings," she said cautiously.

"Let's think about yours and mine right now. Let's take care of us, and deal with them tomorrow." She was touched that he was willing to do that, and this time they took the Deux Chevaux, and she drove. They left the house without even telling the others, but the Morrisons and Donnallys could hear them as they left, and they all sat in the living room looking glum and talking about her.

"I like her," John said plainly, willing to stand up for her to the others. "She's a very nice woman." He looked accusingly at Pascale.

"What do you expect? She's an actress," Pascale stared angrily at her husband. He was defecting to the other side, and she didn't like it, although even she was torn. But she still thought it was a disloyalty to Anne to like Gwen too much. She thought she owed it to Anne to at least not give in too soon, no matter what John said.

"You guys should give the poor woman a break, for Robert's sake, if nothing else," Eric added. It was what he had said that afternoon. And then he turned to his wife. "You've got to admit, she's nice to him."

"She's probably all right, but that doesn't mean she's right for Robert. He needs someone more solid." But what they were really saying was that they wanted him to be alone and mourning Anne forever. They were determined not to make this easy for her, with the exception now of Eric and John.

"Robert doesn't even know what hit him," Diana added pensively. There was no denying that Gwen was impressive. But was she sincere? Diana didn't care if she was, she didn't want to like her. She had dug herself into a hole and refused to budge.

And in town, Robert and Gwen had finally forgotten about them, like naughty children they had left at home. And after a while, they decided to go to one of the open-air cafés in the port, and talk for a while. By then, they were both tired of dancing, although they'd had fun doing it. Robert tried to remember the last time he had gone dancing. Probably at Mike's wedding. He had liked to dance when he was young, but Anne had never been fond of it.

Robert and Gwen talked for hours, sitting at the Gorilla Bar, and admiring the boats docked in the port. It was after two o'clock when they finally got back to the house, and mercifully, everyone was sleeping, and didn't hear them come in.

"Thank you," she whispered as they stood outside his door. "I had a lovely evening."

"So did I," he whispered back, and then he leaned over and kissed her gently on the cheek. Neither of them was ready for more yet, and this was more comfortable for them. "I'll see you tomorrow. Sleep tight," he said, wishing he could tuck her in, but that seemed a crazy thought. She wasn't a child, she was a woman. He just had no idea what to do now, how to begin, how to start a romance with her, particularly under the same roof with his friends. He wasn't even sure if he was ready to yet, and the fact that he was even wondering told him he wasn't.

Instead he watched her close her bedroom door, and closed his own door softly behind him. And the moment he did, he regretted it. But as he had observed about introducing her to the others, this part wasn't easy either. In fact, the whole thing was something of a challenge, but the greatest challenge of all was coming to terms with his memories of Anne, his sense of loyalty to her, and his own conscience. That was the hardest of all, and for the moment he had no idea how to overcome it, and he suspected Gwen didn't either, but it wasn't her problem. It was his to deal with and he knew it. And as he lay in bed that night, thinking first of Anne, and then of Gwen, he couldn't help wondering if she was sleeping, how she looked when she did, what she wore to bed, if anything. There were a lot of things he wanted to find out about her. His mind was still whirling when he went to sleep, and he found he'd been dreaming of her when he woke up the next morning. And as he showered and shaved and dressed, he realized that he couldn't wait to see Gwen.

9

WHEN ROBERT CAME down for breakfast, he found Gwen already there, drinking café au lait and reading the *Herald Tribune,* and there was no one else in sight. They were the first to come downstairs, and she made him a cup of coffee and relinquished the paper to him.

"Did you sleep all right?" She looked interested and concerned about him, and he had to admit he liked that. A lot. It was nice having someone care about him again.

"More or less," he admitted to her. "I dream of Anne sometimes." But he didn't tell Gwen that he hadn't dreamed of his late wife that night, he had dreamed of her, and it had equally disturbed him. The truth was he wanted her, but didn't think he deserved her. He had no right to desert Anne, physically or emotionally, even if she was not there. He wondered what Anne would have thought about it, and if she would have approved. He liked to think she would.

"It was hard for me going out with anyone else, after I divorced my husband," she said simply, as though she understood and didn't want to push him. He liked that about her as well. There was so much about her he did like, more than he had ever expected. "It's hard moving from one life to another. I was only married for nine years, you were married for thirty-eight. How can you possibly expect to move from one life to the next without some stress and introspection and adjustment? It takes time."

"I don't think I've ever thought about it. I never expected to have to do it." Or to love someone else. He didn't dare say that to her.

"Neither did I," she said simply, "but sometimes fate forces us to face the situations we least expect, and most dread." He had never asked her what had happened to end her marriage, but he did now, and she hesitated for an instant. "He had an affair. A very serious affair, with one of our best friends, and I found out about it."

"So you left him?" Robert looked impressed and sorry for her.

"Yes. In about five seconds. I didn't even think about it. I just reacted, and moved out."

"And what did he do?"

"He asked me to come back, he begged me to in fact, and I never spoke to him or discussed it with him. I hated him for a long time, though I don't anymore. But I never forgave him. She was my closest friend, and I blamed both of them. I was pretty rigid in those days."

"Did you ever regret it? Leaving him, I mean."

"Yes. After I did it, I was kicking myself for it, but I never let him know that. I was too proud to. That seemed more important. My ego was bruised, as much as my heart, which was stupid, I guess. Outwardly, I never wavered. I didn't want him to know I still loved him."

"How are you about it now?"

"I'm okay with it. But for a long time I wasn't. I was bitter and angry and destructive at first, and devastated."

"What do you think you should have done? Taken him back?"

She surprised him with her answer. "Probably. Because I don't think we're human, or worthwhile, or worth knowing, if we can't forgive each other. It took me a long time to forgive him. And when I did, it was too late. When it happened, all I wanted was to punish him. So I did. I divorced him. And I realized later I could probably have forgiven him, and lived with it and stayed married. But it was too late then. The same thing could have happened to me, it just didn't. I was in love with him for a long time after we split up. But I couldn't bring myself to forgive him even then. It's something I'll always regret, and it took me a long time to make my peace with it." She looked sad as she said it.

"It must be difficult to have choices about those things," Robert said quietly, "about how far to go, where to draw the line. In some ways, it was easier for me. I didn't have a choice in losing Anne. I just had to live with it. You had choices, and if you allow yourself to, you can blame yourself for a long time for the choice you made. I'm sure you made the right decision in the end."

"I suppose I did. For a long time I wasn't sure. I regretted leaving him terribly afterward, but I was too proud to back down. It cost us both too much in the end. I learned a very painful lesson from it."

"What happened to him?" Something Robert saw in Gwen's eyes made him ask the question.

"After he begged me for several months to come back, and I refused to, eventually, he married the woman he'd been having the affair with. Maybe he would have anyway, but I'm not sure he was in love with her." Her voice grew taut as she said the rest of the words, and it was obvious that she felt a tremendous burden over it. "And then he killed himself six months later. So instead of one life ruined, I destroyed three, hers, mine, and his. I know I'll feel guilty about it forever." She was being honest with him, no matter how painful for her.

"You can't do that to yourself," he said gently. She had

never told him the story, but she had now, and he realized how traumatic the divorce and her ex-husband's death had been for her. "You can't know what else was happening in his life, his head, at the moment. It could have been his own guilt, or about something else."

"I was determined to be tough with him, and not give in," she said sadly. "I was angry that he had cheated on me. But if I had handled it differently, and discussed it with him, maybe not filed for divorce as soon as I did, or at all, we probably would still have been married, and he'd be alive."

"Maybe that wasn't your destiny or his. You can't control what someone else does. Maybe you had finished your life with him."

"No, he did," she said sadly. "In more ways than one. What he did was pretty decisive. He shot himself. His new wife claimed that it was all my fault, that he had never gotten over my divorcing him. She managed to blame me for all of it. And I guess I believed her at the time. I know I have to move on and let go of it, and he's been gone for a while. But I still hesitate about starting anything. I always remind myself of what happened, what could happen again, and my responsibility for it. You can't just walk away from that."

"I think you have to lay that burden down, Gwen," Robert said gently, holding a hand out to her, and taking hers in his own. "You owe it to yourself. You can't punish yourself forever. What he did to you was wrong too. He has a responsibility for this too, more so than you."

She nodded in answer. He had said a lot of good things to her, and she was touched by it. "And what about you? Are you torturing yourself over Anne? Are you feeling that you owe her your life and you shouldn't be happy again? Because if you are, it's a tough spot to be in. You'll need to let yourself off the hook one day too, Robert."

"I will, if I can. She was a powerful force in my life, and a powerful person. I can't imagine her letting me go easily. I think she expected me to be there with her forever. And now she's gone, and I'm here, and I don't know how to move on to the next phase."

"You will. Give it time. You can't rush it." He wasn't. And neither was she, and he was grateful for that too.

"You're an extraordinarily nice person, Gwen," Robert said admiringly.

"Tell your friends that," she teased, and he rolled his eyes just as Eric walked into the kitchen, and interrupted their conversation.

"Have either of you seen Diana?" he inquired, but neither of them had. She hadn't made it to the kitchen yet. But Eric didn't look too worried about it, as he helped himself to a cup of coffee. They had had another fight that morning, about his affair, and she had told him she would never get over it, and would have to divorce him, and he had once again begged her forgiveness, and then eventually lost his temper over her inability to rise above it and forgive him. And once he lost his temper, she stormed out of their bedroom. At that exact moment, she was outside swimming, trying to cope with her feelings of grief and frustration. It hurt all the more because the woman he'd been involved with was so much younger than she was. And as a result, Diana felt finished and unloved and old. For the moment she couldn't regain her feeling of self-worth, nor her love for Eric, who suddenly seemed like a stranger to her.

Eric sat down quietly with Robert and Gwen, and chatted with them. Gwen offered to make them some eggs, but all they wanted were croissants. And when John and Pascale came into the kitchen, she heated the croissants for them, and poured them coffee too.

Diana came in, in a beach towel after that, and ignored Gwen. She acted as though she weren't there. The women were intransigent about her. And even to Robert, it seemed hopeless. If he and Gwen ever developed a serious relationship, he now knew that his best friends could neither sanction it, nor be part of it. It seemed desperately unfair to him, but he couldn't see how to change it, unless they were willing to. He wondered, if she were someone else, if it would be any different. He doubted it, and he was angry at them for their position, or at least Diana and Pascale. He was upset not only for his sake, but for Gwen's. They had never given her a fair chance. He was almost sorry he had let her organize the day for them on the *Talitha G.* If they were going to treat her this way, he thought they didn't deserve it. He was strangely quiet as they finished breakfast, and he suggested to Gwen that they go sailing right after.

"You're upset, aren't you?" she asked him once they were in the sailboat. "Is it what I said this morning about moving on to a new relationship?" She wondered if she had offended him.

"No, it's the way my friends are behaving. The women at least. They're behaving like children, and I'm getting tired of it."

"We have to be patient," she said with more consideration and tolerance than he felt or wanted to give them.

"I'm almost sorry I brought you here," he said sadly. "You don't deserve this." But in a way, it suddenly made the transition easier for him. He wanted to protect her, and he felt loyal to her now as well, not just to Anne. He owed Gwen something too. She had made herself vulnerable to him, and been honest with him. And as they sat in the sailboat side by side, he suddenly pulled her close to him and kissed her hard. It was a feeling of exhilaration and excitement like nothing he had felt in years. And he did it again without coming up for air, and then smiled at her. It had seemed like the only outlet for his anger, and it had definitely been a positive one. His friends' perfidy had only served to bring them closer together in the end.

"Are you okay?" she asked after he'd kissed her, still worried about him, and he grinned at her in answer, looking handsome and young.

"Very much so." And then he kissed her again, and she put her arms around him, and for an instant he forgot where he was, or what he'd been upset about. All he could think of was Gwen, and how extraordinary it was kissing her. He didn't even think about Anne for once. Only Gwen and how much he cared about her.

They sailed silently for a little while, and then she pointed into the distance, and he saw it. The splendid classic motor yacht steaming slowly toward them, with her two big smokestacks and elegant lines. She looked incredibly beautiful, as they glanced first at her, and then smiled at each other. It was one of those moments they both knew they'd remember for a long time.

"You make me very happy." Robert smiled at her, she had brought fresh excitement into his life, and a feeling he hadn't experienced in years. He could hardly wait to spend the day on the boat with her, and he was only sorry he had invited the others. But they dutifully sailed back to put the sailboat away, and tell his friends that the yacht was approaching. And without thinking, he walked up the path with her, hand in hand. He had never felt as comfortable in his life, not even with Anne. She had been cooler and less demonstrative. But everything about Gwen was gentle and soft and warm.

He went upstairs to get his bathing suit and a few things when he got back to the house, and then, he went to her bedroom to find Gwen. She was wearing a white cotton sundress, and her hair framed her face, as she turned and smiled at him. He took her in his arms again, and kissed her, and he felt neither guilt nor sorrow this time. He felt relief, and peace, and deep affection. He didn't know her well yet, but he knew he had found a woman who could mean a great deal to him. There was so much he liked about her. And without saying a word, they went downstairs hand in hand, in bold defiance of his friends. Gwen was prepared to be discreet about it, but he made it clear to her, and to them, that this was what he wanted, and who he had become. And for now at least, he expected them to accept and respect the changes in him, but Gwen as well, and pay the consequences if they didn't.

10

THEIR DAY ON *Talitha G* with Henry Adams and his wife Cherie proved to be more fun and far more glamorous than any of Robert's group had expected or dreamed. Henry was charming to everyone, and so good looking that all Pascale and Diana could do was stare at him, and he made a huge fuss over all of them, and made certain that the crew did as well. They were assigned cabins to change their clothes, Cherie and Pascale and Diana became fast friends, and the superstar supermodel of Paris and New York runways spent the afternoon flirting with John. He looked like he had died and gone to heaven.

The lunch that was prepared for them was fabulous, and afterward they all lay in the sun, in abject comfort and opulence. And by the time the day was over, Gwen was no more appealing to Diana and Pascale, but her movie star friends were. Diana whispered to Pascale, as they lay in comfortable deck chairs, that it was a life one could easily get accustomed to, and they were surprised that Gwen was willing to stay with Robert, in their crumbling villa. It was obvious that she was greatly admired by all these handsome men. They made a huge fuss over her, but she treated them all like brothers or friends. It was clear to everyone how much she cared about Robert and no one else, much to Diana and Pascale's chagrin. She turned her full attention to him, and saw to it that he was comfortable and content and treated well. Had either of the other two women been fair, they would have been thrilled for him. But at least Eric and John were.

They had dinner in the dining saloon that night, anchored outside the Port of St Tropez, as they watched sailboats glide by on the way home from pleasure cruises and races. And a number of smaller craft circled them, just to admire the handsome yacht, and see who was on board. And several tourists, and a couple of well-informed paparazzi snapped pictures of them. They seemed to know who was on every yacht on the Riviera. And this one was a huge prize for them, with five stars on board, drinking champagne, and wearing bikinis and thongs. Cherie Adams went topless all afternoon, but Gwen was cautious and wore her top. She knew only too well what the tabloids would have done with photographs like that.

Gwen and Robert looked happy and relaxed, and they sat

together and spoke in low tones, when they weren't laughing with their hosts, playing cards or liar's dice, or holding hands quietly as they looked out over the Mediterranean, lost in their own thoughts, or standing very near each other. Pascale and Diana glanced at them from time to time, and Pascale kept insisting it was a life Robert would never adjust to, or want. It was too jet set for him, particularly when you thought of the sensible life he had shared with Anne. They just weren't that kind of people, but Robert certainly seemed to be enjoying it, and was just as comfortable talking to Henry and the other two major actors on board, or to Henry's incredible-looking wife, as he was with the comfortable old friends he had brought with him.

Eric was clearly impressed by Cherie, as was John, and she nearly rendered them speechless when she had taken off her top and continued chatting with them. It was certainly the custom in France, but none of the men had been prepared for the effect it would have on them.

By dinnertime, they were all extremely comfortable with each other, and as the tender finally took them back to Coup de Foudre, Diana said she felt like Cinderella as she watched the footmen turn back into mice, and the coach into a pumpkin.

"Wow! What a day!" Pascale was staring into space dreamily as the crew member from *Talitha G* helped her from the tender onto their tiny dock. All three actors on board had made a fuss over her, and she hated to leave.

She could hardly wait to tell her mother whom she had met, and what yacht she'd been on. She felt like Queen for a Day.

"Kind of knocks your socks off, doesn't it?" Eric said to John as he poured them all a glass of wine in the living room of the villa. "That's quite a life you lead," he said to Gwen, admiring her more for not playing star. Seeing her with her friends had somehow brought it into perspective for them. But Robert liked that about her, the fact that she was just as comfortable with his friends as her own, and had no sense of self-importance. He had realized that the very first time he met her, and the time he had spent with her since had confirmed it to him.

For once Pascale and Diana had very little to say, and the way they looked at her seemed subtly changed. They had by no means accepted her, just because she knew a lot of movie stars, but they were willing to acknowledge, at least privately, that there might be more to her than they had at first suspected. And there was no denying that Robert looked very happy. But they still felt an overwhelming need to protect him. From what, they were no longer quite as sure, but they were both equally convinced that she couldn't possibly be as nice and sincere as she appeared to be. But it was harder now to assign an evil motive to her. There was really no reason for her to be with Robert, except that she genuinely cared for him.

She and Robert went out for a drink in town that

night, at the Gorilla Bar, and they stopped in for a few minutes at the disco, and on the way home, he kissed her again as he had before, and thanked her for the wonderful day she'd given all of them, by introducing them to her friends, and he laughed as he remembered how John had looked when Cherie took off her top.

"That's a pretty racy crowd you run in," he commented, and she nodded with a grin, and looked even younger than she was.

"They're a lot of fun, in small doses." The ones they had seen that day were all good friends of hers, but a lot of the Hollywood crowd didn't appeal to her. There was a great deal more substance to her. "You need more than that to make life interesting, I'm afraid. And if you let it, it really spoils you." And clearly, in his eyes, at least, it hadn't done that. He admired her enormously for who she was.

"You're not bored with these old friends of mine?" If nothing else, they were all considerably older than she was, and their lives were far more mundane. Particularly his, he felt. Robert was sane enough not to see himself as a romantic figure. But far more important, she did. Very much so. She had never met anyone who impressed her as much, whom she admired as much, and she had already realized, before she came to St Tropez, that she was falling in love with him. And the good news was that he seemed to reciprocate her feelings.

"I like your friends," she said comfortably, as they

drove home. "I don't think they like me much, but maybe they'll get over it. I think they just want to be loyal to Anne. Maybe in time, they'll figure out that I'm not trying to step on anyone's toes, I just love being with you." She smiled at him, and he leaned over again and kissed her.

"You make me feel very lucky," he said. He still wrestled with himself about Anne sometimes, and how much he had loved her, how different she was from Gwen, and how many wonderful years they had spent together. But she was gone, no matter how much he regretted it. And he was trying to tell himself that he had a right to someone in his life, even if not someone as dazzling as Gwen. He couldn't imagine that she would want to be with him for very long. If nothing else, he was twenty-two years older than she was, which seemed a lot to him, if not to her. She had never seemed daunted by his age.

"I'm the lucky one," Gwen said as they drove along in her car in the moonlight. "You're intelligent, fun to be with, incredibly handsome, and one of the nicest people I've ever met," she said as she glanced over at him, and he smiled sheepishly.

"Just how much have you been drinking?" he teased.

She laughed at him, and touched his arm, as they bounced along the rutted driveway, and a moment later, he stopped the car, took her in his arms, and kissed her properly, and then they walked inside the house, hand in hand, trying not to make any sound so as not to wake the others, who were all sleeping. He left her in front of her room, with a lingering kiss, and when he went to his own room, he stopped and stared at the photograph of Anne he had put on his bed table. He wondered what she would think of this, if she would think him an old fool, or wish him well. He wasn't quite sure. He wasn't even sure how he felt about it. But when he didn't ponder it too much, he had to admit, he was happier with Gwen than he could ever have believed possible. But he constantly had to remind himself that it wouldn't go anywhere, and it was just a fun phase of his life that the others would tease him about in years to come, and he would long remember.

And when he went to bed that night, he lay wondering what Gwen was thinking and doing in her room. He was aching to knock on her door and kiss her again, but he didn't dare, and he was still afraid to allow himself to do more than kiss her. He knew that if he did more than that, he would feel Anne watching him. And the last thing he wanted to do was betray either of them.

He fell asleep and dreamed of both of them, in a tangled dream where he saw Anne and Gwen walking through a garden with their arms around each other, and his friends were all pointing accusing fingers at him, and shouting something unintelligible at him. It was a troubling dream, and he awoke several times. And when he went back to sleep, he dreamed of Mandy. She was holding her mother's photograph and looking sorrowfully at him.

"I really miss her," she said softly.

"So do I," he said, crying in the dream. And when he awoke this time, his face was wet with tears. He lay in bed for a long time after that, thinking of Anne, and then of Gwen.

And he was startled when he heard a knock on the door. He pulled on a pair of khaki pants, and was surprised to see Gwen. It was still early, and he hadn't heard the others get up.

"Good morning," Gwen said softly. "Did you sleep all right? I don't know why, but I was worried about you." They were standing in the hall whispering, and she looked beautiful in a white nightgown and robe and bare feet.

"I had weird dreams about you and Anne walking in a garden." She looked startled when he said it.

"That's weird, so did I. I was awake for a long time last night, thinking about you," she said softly, as she looked up at him. He looked handsome and rugged with uncombed hair.

"I thought about you too. Maybe we should have visited each other," he said softly, so no one would hear him.

He loved feeling Gwen near him, as she stood next to him and smiled at him. "I'll take a shower and meet you at breakfast in ten minutes."

And when he appeared, he looked immaculate and perfectly shaved, in shorts and a T-shirt. She was wearing little white shorts and a halter top, which paled in comparison to Agathe's latest creation when she appeared. She was wearing a pink tulle bra with little rosebuds on it, and pink hot pants, and Eric commented when he came in that she looked like one of her French poodles. They were beginning to enjoy waiting to see what she would wear every day, and how outlandish it would be. She never disappointed them, and she didn't that morning as they chatted before the others got up. It was nice having time by themselves. The others grinned as they walked into the kitchen for breakfast too. Agathe was more entertaining than television.

There was a call for Eric, just as Diana walked into the room, it was from the States, and an operator told Pascale that it was person to person. He frowned, and then went into the next room to answer it, which didn't go unnoticed by his wife. But he looked relaxed and unconcerned when he came back to the kitchen ten minutes later. Diana was watching him closely.

"One of my partners," he explained to the room at large, and Diana concentrated on her croissants and took a long sip of her coffee as though it were whiskey. In the thirty-two years of their marriage, none of his partners had ever called him on vacation. She knew exactly who it was, and right after breakfast, she accused him of it.

"It was Barbara, wasn't it?" The woman he had had the affair with. He hesitated for a long moment, and then nodded. He didn't want to lie to her. "Why did she call you?"

"Why do you think?" he said, looking upset, as they stood in the living room. They didn't want the others to hear them. "This isn't easy for her either."

"And if I leave you, will you marry her?" It was what she was really worried about now. She wondered if they had only taken a time-out to see if his marriage would fall apart, or if they had truly ended it, as Eric had told her before they left New York.

"Of course not. Diana, I'm thirty years older than she is. And that isn't even the point. I love you. I made a mistake, I did something incredibly stupid. I was wrong. I've admitted it. Now let it die, for chrissake. Let's leave it behind us, and go on."

"That's easy for you to say," she said, looking at him with ravaged eyes. She couldn't get over it. She had been betrayed and rejected. And now she felt a thousand years old, and she no longer trusted him. It didn't help that she was old enough to be the woman's mother. For the first time in her life, she felt old and unattractive to him. He had tried to make love to her several times since they'd been there, but Diana had refused to. She just couldn't. She didn't know if she ever would again.

"I don't know what to say to you anymore. I guess it'll just take time for you to trust me again." And in the meantime, he knew he had to be patient, and pay for his sins, but it wasn't easy for either of them. And Barbara was begging him to come back to her. She had conned the number out of his secretary, who felt sorry for her. He had just reminded her that it was impossible, and asked her not to call him again. She was crying when they hung up, and he felt like a monster. But he could hardly complain to his wife about it. They both hated him. It was a miserable situation for him, but he also recognized that it was his own fault.

And just as Eric and Diana stopped talking, Gwen walked in, looking happy and relaxed, and then instantly awkward as she saw the look of distress on their faces. It was easy to see that something terrible was happening to them, and she didn't want to intrude. Diana looked no closer to reconciliation with him than she had when they arrived in St Tropez, although they had shared a few pleasant moments. But the truth haunted her, no matter how pretty St Tropez was, how good the dinners, or how lovely the moonlight, he had betrayed her, and nothing would allow her to forget it. It was why she had told

Pascale the night she arrived that she thought she had to divorce him. Because she could no longer imagine getting over it or forgiving him, and all it took was one phone call to remind her of the agony he'd put her through.

"I'm sorry, I didn't mean to interrupt you," Gwen said, hastening through the room, and Robert followed a moment later. He stopped to ask Eric a question.

"Do you want to come sailing with us?" Robert asked easily, oblivious to the look of torment on their faces. He thought it was the usual minor marital dispute about who was going swimming and who was going shopping. The Donnallys hadn't told him about the problem the Morrisons were having, and he was entirely unaware of it.

"Sure," Eric said quickly, relieved to get out of the discussion he'd been having with Diana. "I'll put my suit on."

"Diana, do you want to come too?" Robert extended the invitation to her, but she declined just as quickly as Eric had agreed.

"Pascale and I are going to the market," she said, and walked away. And when he asked John, when he found him, coming out of his bedroom, with the dismembered toilet handle in his hand again, John said he was going to stick around the house and make some phone calls to his office.

And much to Robert's surprise and disappointment,

Gwen decided to stay home too. She said she had a headache, but after the look she'd seen on Eric's face, she thought the two men might need some time together on their own. There were some letters she wanted to write anyway, and Robert kissed her before he left with Eric to take out the sailboat.

The house was very quiet, as she sat in the living room, writing notes and postcards, and she could hear John talking on the phone, and smell cigar smoke wafting toward her from the kitchen. She didn't mind it, and she loved the sounds of the birds in the garden. It was a peaceful place, despite its flaws and obvious decay, and she was happy she had come.

John had stopped talking for quite a while, when she went out to the kitchen to make herself another cup of coffee, and what she saw was his lifeless form slumped over the table. He still had the phone in his hand, and the line had gone dead eventually, as he lay facedown on his papers. It took her less than a fraction of a second to absorb what she was seeing, and she ran to him, shook him, and called his name, and then laid him on the floor as gently as she could to check his breathing. He was barely breathing and his pulse was faint, and she knew that there was no one in the house to help her. She had no idea where the French couple had gone, and all the others were out, either sailing or at the market. She was alone.

"John! John!" she called out to him again, and as she gently shook him, she saw his breathing stop and his face turn gray. She had no idea what had happened to him, and then as though looking for a clue, she glanced up at the table. There was a plate of neatly cut little sausages, and she suddenly wondered if he had choked, or had a heart attack. But the only thing she could think of to do was the Heimlich maneuver. She had learned it years before, along with CPR, and wasn't even sure she remembered the fine points of it. But it was no easy thing to do with him lying flat on his back on the floor, and unconscious. John was a powerfully built man and heavy for her. But she had dragged him out of his chair and onto the floor, which took all her strength.

She swept his mouth with her fingers, but found nothing there, and then gave him three short breaths, but it was obvious his airway was blocked. It was like breathing into a wall. She straddled his body then, and using both hands interlocked, she pressed his abdomen, and prayed.

His lips had begun turning blue, and there was no 911 to call, as she continued doing it, and praying that he wouldn't die before she could help him. Her own desperation only made her do it sharply again and again and suddenly there was a pop, he gave a hideous choking sound, and a piece of sausage like a champagne cork flew out of his mouth, and landed on the kitchen floor, six feet from where she was kneeling over him. She turned him on his side, and he instantly threw up, and lay gasping on the floor, but at least he was breathing. The piece of sausage lodged in his throat had very nearly killed him. And it was several minutes before he rolled himself onto his back, and lay looking up at her.

"I choked," he said weakly.

"I know. How do you feel now?" She was looking very worried.

"Kind of dizzy," he said softly. "I was smoking a cigar and talking, and I ate one of those pieces of sausage. It got stuck and I couldn't make a sound," he said, remembering how desperate he had felt, and he still looked frightened. He was shaking and pale.

"Why don't I take you to the hospital?" she offered, as she cleaned up the remains of his breakfast, and then wiped his face with a cool, damp cloth, as he looked gratefully at her.

"Thanks, Gwen. You saved my life." It was true, and they both knew it. He would have died within minutes, or suffered permanent brain damage if it had taken her any longer to dislodge it. "I'm okay now. I just need to catch my breath a little."

"Are you sure? Maybe Eric can take a look at you when he gets back from the boat." She picked up the piece of sausage then, it was about the size of a wine cork, and she saved it in a dish towel to show to Eric, or the hospital, if he let her take him, which he wouldn't.

She helped him back into the chair, and she offered him a glass of water, but he only sipped it. And she saw with relief that the color in his face had returned. As frightening as it had been, the emergency was over. "Thank God you were here," he said gratefully. "Why didn't you go with the others?" He looked almost normal by then, though somewhat shaken by the experience. It had been terrifying strangling and then losing consciousness. He had been sure, as she had been when she found him, that he was dying.

"I thought maybe Eric wanted to talk to Robert, and the ladies didn't look too excited to have me join them."

"They'll get over it," he said, patting her hand. "Anne was their best friend. It's hard watching him with someone else, but he's lucky to have you," he said fairly. "We all are. Give us a chance, Gwen, we'll get there." He had been nice to her right from the beginning, and Eric had come around, but the women had been a lot slower to tolerate her. The day on *Talitha G* had helped, but they were still making up their minds about her, unlike Robert, who already knew what a decent person she was and how much he liked her.

She and John were still sitting in the kitchen talking when Robert and Eric walked in two hours later. John had showered and changed his shirt and come back to sit with Gwen. They had talked about life and friends and loss, and Robert. John thought the world of him, and wanted only the best for him, as they all did.

"Well, you missed it," John said jovially as they walked in, but Gwen had noticed that he hadn't lit a cigar since it had happened, he was still feeling somewhat shaken, and she was relieved to see Eric. "I tried to commit suicide on a piece of pork. That's how they do it over here. But like everything else in this country, it didn't work. As a matter of fact, Gwen saved my life."

"What's all that?" Robert laughed as he heard it. He had no idea what John was talking about. And Eric looked instantly serious. He had been telling Robert about what was happening to him and Diana, it was why Gwen hadn't gone sailing with them, so they could do just that, and it was obviously destiny that she hadn't gone with them. If she had, they would have found John dead in the kitchen when they returned.

"I'm serious," John said, looking gratefully at Gwen, and then explained it to them. Both men looked impressed by what had almost happened.

"I saved the sausage to show you," Gwen said quietly, and handed the dish towel to Eric so he could see it. He was horrified when he looked at it, and then back at John.

"That's just about the right size to plug up your windpipe and kill you." And then he glanced at Gwen and thanked her for her wits and persistence. "How about smaller bites next time?" he said to John, and then went to get the stethoscope he'd brought, so he could check him. But when he did, John's blood pressure and heart seemed fine, and to prove it, he lit a cigar, just as Pascale and Diana returned from the market. He was still wearing the blood pressure cuff when he lit it, and Pascale looked confused at the scene in the kitchen, as she glanced from Eric to John.

"What kind of games have you all been playing?" she scolded.

"Gwen offered to take off the top of her bathing suit, and Eric was checking to see how it affected me," John said with a broad grin as Gwen objected and his wife shook her head in disapproval.

"Very cute," she said, setting down their baskets. "Is something wrong?" she asked, noticing the serious faces of the others.

"He choked on a piece of sausage," Eric said simply, "and it damn near killed him. Gwen did the Heimlich on him, and she saved him. That's it in a nutshell." And to impress Pascale with the seriousness of it, and Gwen's act of heroism, "He was unconscious when she found him."

"*Mon Dieu,* but how did that happen?" She looked terrified as she looked at John, glanced gratefully at Gwen, and put her arms around him. "Are you all right? What were you doing?"

"Talking, smoking, and eating. Gwen's a good kid. I'd have been up the creek, permanently, without her." Pascale could see in his eyes, despite the bluster, that he'd really been frightened, and she went over to hug Gwen then.

"Thank you . . . I don't know what to say . . . thank you." Pascale was choked with emotion as Gwen hugged her back. She was just glad to have been there. They had been lucky.

"When's lunch?" John said with a broad grin, as Pascale rolled her eyes and groaned.

"I bought *boudin noir* at the market, but no more sausages for you. I'm going to give you baby food until you learn how to eat properly." He didn't disagree with her, and he put an arm around his wife and kissed her. It was as though he had been given the gift of life, unexpectedly, and perhaps undeservedly, but he was grateful for it.

The group was lively at lunch that day, and everyone was in good spirits, even Eric and Diana. It was as though they had all been saved, by the hand of fate, from another disaster. And John seemed particularly happy. He and Pascale went up to their room afterward, for a nap, and Eric asked Diana to go for a walk with him, which left Robert and Gwen to their own devices. They walked outside, and lay on the little dock, soaking up the sunshine.

She told him everything that happened with John, and he shook his head, listening, remembering the night he had found Anne, and reliving the nightmare without saying so to her.

"John is damn lucky you found him."

"I'm glad I did," she said softly, still a little awestruck by all that had happened, and then Robert looked at her with surprising tenderness.

"I'm glad I found you, Gwen. I'm not sure I'm ready for you, or that I deserve you. But I have a lot of strong feelings for you." It was a timid way of telling her he was falling in love with her, but she was also falling in love with him, and being there together in the South of France, with his friends, was drawing them even closer together. "Life is strange, isn't it? It never even occurred to me that I'd lose Anne. I thought she'd outlive me. I never ever thought there would be anyone else in my life again. And Eric was telling me some very upsetting things today about them. Just when you think you have a sure thing in your hand, it all falls apart, and you have to start at the beginning. And then when you think your life is over, it starts again, and you get another chance. Maybe that's what makes life worth living."

"I never thought I'd find anyone that important to me again," Gwen concurred. "I thought I'd made enough mistakes and used up all my tickets. But maybe not," she said softly, looking at him.

They sat quietly together for a long time, looking out at the water, contemplating both their past, and their future.

"I love you, Gwen," he said, turning to look at her. "I can't believe I'd be right for you. I'm too old, our lives are very different. But who knows, maybe this is the best thing that ever happened to either of us." He smiled peacefully as he put an arm around her. "Let's just see what happens."

"I love you too," she whispered, looking up at him, and then, he kissed her, as the sun shone brightly over St Tropez.

11

FROM THE TIME Gwen saved John from choking, everyone's attitudes seemed to subtly change toward her. It wasn't immediate or overt, it was more of a gradual thing, but it was palpable, as the others made small efforts toward her. The next time Pascale and Diana went to the market, they asked her to join them. They talked to her cautiously at first, and then began to open up and chat more comfortably around her. She carried groceries with them, cooked breakfast for everyone, and cleaned the kitchen for Pascale at night. And when Pascale felt sick one night, Gwen cooked dinner for the others, and made chicken soup for Pascale. She had eaten bad clams at the port, and got violently ill, and as it turned out, she felt sick for days after.

She felt so ill eventually that Eric was afraid she might have contracted salmonella or hepatitis, and he wanted her to see a local doctor and get some blood work, but Pascale insisted she was fine, and stayed in bed for a few days.

By the end of the first week Gwen was there, Diana was speaking openly in front of her, and she had even admitted Eric's recent affair to her. Gwen was quiet about it at first, and then couldn't restrain herself any longer.

"I don't have any right to tell you this, Diana. And I don't know what you should do. But my husband had an affair when we were married, and I walked out on him the day I found out. I shut him out, I closed the door, I never talked to him again. I filed for a divorce. We'd been married for nine years, and I think in a way I forced him to marry the woman he'd had the affair with. I'm not sure he would have if I hadn't walked out. I don't know what happened after that, or why he did it. I never took his calls, or saw him. But he committed suicide six months after he married her, and afterward she said that he had always been in love with me. And the stupid thing, the really sinful, awful part, is that I was still in love with him. I'm not saying that Eric would ever do anything like that, but what I am saying is that I wasted my marriage, I threw it away. At the time, I thought I could never forgive him, and she was my best friend. But I do know I made a terrible mistake and I wish I hadn't done it. Be smarter than I was," Gwen said with tears in her eyes, as Diana listened to her carefully, touched by what Gwen was saying to her. "It's all right to be hurt and angry, but don't throw it all away." Diana nodded, as they dried the dishes, and when Eric walked into the room, she turned away. It was an awful story, but there was a lesson to be learned, not about suicide, but about loving someone and forgiving them, and not cutting off your nose to spite your face. And that night, Gwen told Robert what she had said.

"I'm glad you did. I've been trying to get Eric to hang in too. He's pretty discouraged, and I guess she's pretty angry at him, but that's understandable. If they can just get through this part, and love each other in spite of it, maybe they'll wind up with something even better in the end. Eric isn't sure Diana will stick it out." And neither was Gwen, from everything Diana had said.

Gwen cooked breakfast for all of them in Pascale's place the next day, she was feeling too weak from the remainder of her food poisoning to get out of bed, and when John joined them in the kitchen, he looked concerned.

"I don't like the way she looks," he said quietly to Eric over breakfast. "She doesn't want to admit it, but I can tell she still feels pretty sick. I think she should see a doctor here in St Tropez and maybe get some tests."

"I'll take a look at her after breakfast," Eric offered, and John thanked him, and after they ate Gwen's French toast, Eric disappeared upstairs. Pascale told him that she thought it was a combination of problems, and she shared her concerns with him. Everything she said sounded reasonable, and he was able to reassure John when he came back downstairs.

"I think she just feels lousy, it takes a while to get over a really bad case of food poisoning like that." But John wasn't convinced, and nagged her again about going to the doctor, when he checked on her. She said she hated the doctors in France.

"And so do you," she reminded him. But when he looked at her, he thought she looked green.

And when the entire group met again for lunch, including Pascale, who said she felt better, Robert and Gwen were talking about extending their trip by another week.

"Hurray!" Diana said, and then looked embarrassed, but a look of budding friendship passed between her and Gwen. They were all slowly discovering that she was not only decent, but a lovely person, and they were less worried about Robert than they had been. She was beginning to restore their faith in his judgment, and John was excited for him. He said as much to Pascale that afternoon.

"Look at the life he could have with her, Pascale. It's pretty exciting. A movie star? At his age, it'll put some real spark in his life."

"He doesn't need that," Pascale said cautiously. Although she was grateful for what Gwen had done for John when he was choking, she still wanted to be sure that

Robert wasn't making a mistake, if it even got that far. But only time would tell. "He needs a real person, a companion, a good friend."

"She is a real person. Look at her, she's done more cooking and cleaning around here than Diana or you. She's nice to all of us, she put up with all your bullshit in the beginning, and she was a good sport about it. And the most important thing is that I think she loves him. And he loves her."

"You don't think he'd marry her, do you?" Pascale still looked concerned.

"At our age, who needs to get married? He's not going to have kids. All they need is to have a good time together. I think that's all either of them wants."

"Good," she said, looking relieved.

"And what about you? Are you going to be reasonable and go to the doctor? I don't care if you feel better, you might have picked up some really nasty bug. Maybe you need antibiotics."

"All I need is sleep." She was so exhausted, she could hardly get out of bed suddenly, and she spent the entire morning every day waiting for afternoon to come so she could take a nap. She was still sleeping at five o'clock that afternoon when Eric, Robert, and Gwen came back from a sail. Diana was lying on a deck chair in the garden, reading, and John had gone to the nearest hotel to send a fax to New York.

"How was your sail?" Diana asked with a slow smile, as she glanced at Eric. She had been thinking about him all afternoon, and some of the things Gwen had said. She was still angry at him, but she could conceive of the possibility that one day, her hurt and disappointment might actually diminish. She had been thinking of some of the things they'd done over the years, the things she loved about him, and although she hated him for what he'd done, she could almost understand it. Maybe it was a last grab at his youth. She wasn't entirely sure she could blame him for that. And when he looked at her, he paused for an instant. For the first time, he had seen something different in her eyes.

"It was nice," he said, and as he walked past her, she moved her legs on her deck chair, and he stopped for an instant, and then sat down. "I missed you today," he said hesitantly, as the others went back into the house. "I was thinking all afternoon, while we sailed."

"So was I," she said without elaborating, but he could sense that some of the ice had melted from around her heart.

"I really want to work this out. I know I was wrong. And I can't expect you to believe me or trust me again so soon. But I'd like to think you will again in time."

"I'd like to think that too," she said honestly. Their friends had talked to both of them, but what Gwen had said to her had touched her most. Her words had been heavily weighted by the pain her own mistakes had caused. And it was obvious that she had carried the burden of regret ever since. "We'll see" was all Diana could promise him now.

But when they went back to their room late that afternoon, she seemed to have a lighter step, and when Eric said something funny to her, she laughed.

"Do you want to go out to dinner tonight?" Eric asked her, and she thought about it for a minute and then nodded.

"What do you suppose the others want to do?"

"Let's just go out the two of us for a change. They can manage for themselves." Eric was so relieved to be talking to her again. The tides had turned.

Pascale decided to stay in bed and sleep, and John had gotten a package of papers from his office and wanted to do some reading. And Robert and Gwen decided to walk around St Tropez and have something to eat at the port.

They were sitting at the Gorilla Bar again late that night, talking and laughing, when he looked at Gwen and took her hand, and without further explanation, he said, "Come on, let's go home."

"Are you tired?" She was startled by his suddenly wanting to go back, but he seemed happy and in good spirits, and they paid the check, and drove back to the villa in her Deux Chevaux.

The house was quiet when they got there. Eric and

Diana were still out, and John and Pascale's lights were out and they had gone to bed. Gwen and Robert whispered like teenagers as they came up the stairs.

"Good night," she said, as he kissed her, but he hesitated for a long time before leaving her. And then he looked at her and felt like a kid.

"I was wondering if . . . I thought maybe . . . do you want to sleep in my room tonight, Gwen?" he asked softly, blushing in the dark.

"I'd love that." They had proceeded thus far with great caution, and had felt no pressure to go farther than they felt able to at the time. But things suddenly felt different to him, he knew they were both ready, and for the past few days he had felt oddly at peace about Anne. He had had a dream the night before where she had been laughing and smiling and waving at him, and she kissed him good-bye. He didn't know where she was going, and he was crying when he woke up, but they were tears of relief and not grief. Somehow, he had the feeling that she was all right. And he had described the dream to Gwen.

He put a single light on in his room, and Gwen walked in behind him slowly, and saw the photograph of Anne on his bed table, and for an instant it touched her heart. It was so sad to think that he had had a loving companion for so long, and now he was alone. But he had his children, and his memories of the life they'd shared. And now he had Gwen. He had a lot.

He stood looking at Gwen for a long moment, as though savoring what they were about to share, and then ever so gently he held out his hand. She took two steps toward him and put her arms around him. She wanted to take away all the hurt that he had felt, and comfort the loss.

"I love you, Robert," she whispered, "everything's going to be all right." He nodded, and there were tears in his eyes as he kissed her, tears of good-bye to Anne, and of love for Gwen. And then slowly, they were enveloped in their passion, their kisses seemed to devour them, and moments later they were lying on his bed. He already knew, from seeing her in a bikini, how spectacular her body would be, but it was not only that he hungered for now, it was her heart.

And when afterward they lay in each other's arms, sated, sleepy, content, he held her close to him, and she looked up at him and smiled. "You make me so happy," she said, and meant it. He pulled her closer to him, unable to find words for a moment. She was one of the great gifts of his life.

12

THE NEXT MORNING, when they came out of Robert's room to go down to breakfast, they ran into Diana, who was looking worried. She had just stopped in to see Pascale, who was violently ill again, and John had already made an appointment for her at a local doctor. He was no longer willing to listen to her insisting she was all right. Clearly, she was not.

"What do you think it is?" Gwen asked Eric over breakfast. Diana had made them all scrambled eggs that day.

"I'm not sure. I think she may have picked up some kind of nasty bacterial infection. She needs antibiotics, before she winds up in the hospital. They may admit her for a few days anyway. She's getting dehydrated from throwing up." But he didn't look as worried as John.

And after breakfast, when Robert and Gwen went into town to mail some letters, Diana turned to her husband with a knowing smile. "Who do you think I saw

219

coming out of Robert's room this morning with a big grin on her face?"

He looked amused by the question, and pretended to think about it. "Let's see . . . hm . . . Agathe?"

"Yeah, sure." They had come home late themselves the night before. They had had a lovely evening, a good dinner, and had even gone dancing. It was the first bridge back from the nightmare where they'd been for the past two months. They still had a long road back to safety, but they had started back at last.

"No, it was Gwen," Diana said triumphantly, as though she had approved of her all along.

"That's too bad. I sort of hoped it was Agathe. It would be so much fun to see what outfits she'd take with her to New York. I'm glad they're happy," he said, looking serious again. "They both deserve it." Like the others in the group, he had come to like her, and Robert had never looked as well. It had been seven months since Anne had died, a long, sad time for him. And by some standards, he had gotten back into life fairly quickly, but Eric knew that those things can't be measured. And whatever was right for Robert was acceptable to him. "She's a nice woman, and he's a good man."

"I wonder what his kids will think about it," Diana said pensively, as Eric shrugged.

"He's a grown man, he has a right to do what he wants."

"His kids may not agree with that."

"Then they'd better get used to it. He has a right to a life. Anne would have wanted that for him." Diana nodded, and knew that that much was true. Anne had been practical and sensible to a fault. "Just because he's with Gwen doesn't mean he's forgotten Anne. The kids should get that in time." Diana nodded again, as John came into the room. He and Eric had discussed it at length, and John was taking Pascale to the doctor, and said he hoped they'd be back in time for lunch. Eric wanted her to be seen by a local internist and to get a battery of tests.

"Do you want me to come with you?" Diana volunteered, but John said they'd be fine. Or at least he hoped Pascale would be, once they gave her some medicine. And Eric and Diana were relieved to see that, no matter how rotten she felt, she didn't actually look that bad. It was obviously just a bug. Although John had an unspoken terror that it might be something worse, and once they got home, he wanted their doctor to go over her with a fine-toothed comb. But they were all leaving in another week, and the medicine should hold her till then. He didn't have much faith in French doctors, or in anything in France.

And he regaled Pascale with his hatred of all things French on their way to the doctor. By the time they got there, she was ready to strangle him. And while they were waiting for the doctor, she threw up again and started to cry, which completely unnerved John.

"I feel so awful," she said mournfully. "I've been sick for a week."

"I know, baby. We'll get some medicine for you, and you'll be fine." And as they sat there, waiting, he even thought about taking her home to New York.

They ushered her in to an examining room finally, took her vital signs, looked into her eyes and at her tongue. They took her blood pressure, and weighed her, and a nurse in a ragged white dress and sandals wrote it all down. Nurses in France were not as pristine as in New York, but Pascale was used to it and didn't care as much as John.

And when the doctor saw her finally, he asked her a long list of questions, nodded a lot, jotted some things down, and drew some blood, and then told Pascale he'd call her at home. He told her he didn't want to give her any medication until he reviewed the test results. And she left, knowing as little as she had when she'd come.

"What did he say?" John asked worriedly when she emerged finally. She'd been gone for more than an hour, and he'd been worried sick about her.

"Not much," she said honestly. "He said he'd call me when he got the results."

"Results of what?" John looked panicked.

"He took some blood."

"That's it? That's all? What kind of moron is he? Eric said he should give you antibiotics. Let me talk to him."

He was ready to attack the nurse at the desk, but Pascale insisted that they go home.

"He's not going to give me anything till he gets the results. That makes sense. He thought it might be salmonella. I may have to come back and give them some samples, depending on what he finds in my blood."

"Oh for chrissake, Pascale. This is a third world country."

"No, it's not," she said, looking insulted, "it's my home. You can insult my mother if you want, but not France. *Ça, c'est trop!*" That's too much! But he was still complaining loudly all the way back to the car. And when they got back to the villa, he told Eric what a fool he thought the doctor was.

"Why don't you just prescribe something for her?" John looked at him with pleading eyes, but Eric shook his head.

"I don't think they'd even honor my script here, and to be honest with you, John, he's right. He shouldn't give her anything till he knows what she's got. It won't take long."

"The hell it won't. This is France."

But as it turned out, the nurse called Pascale the next day. The doctor wanted to see her again, and they had time for her that afternoon. John wanted to go with her, but Pascale said she was fine. She actually felt better than she had the day before. And in the end, Gwen went with her, she wanted to do some errands in town, and the two women drove off in the Deux Chevaux. And it was nearly dinnertime when they got home. John was worried sick by then, but both Gwen and Pascale looked happy, and confessed that they'd gone shopping after Pascale saw the doctor, which hadn't taken long.

"You could have called at least!" John scolded Pascale, and then asked her what the doctor had done, and she said not much. He said she was fine.

"Did he give you antibiotics this time?" He looked more furious by the minute. He had really been worried about her all afternoon, and she herself realized now that she should have called, but she had had a good time with Gwen, and she thought John would be busy with their friends. As it turned out, he had sat in the house all after-noon waiting for her.

"He said I don't need antibiotics. It'll take care of it-self," she said simply, anxious to show Diana what she and Gwen had bought. They'd found a new dress shop and nearly bought them out.

"I think this doctor is a complete asshole," John said in a total fury, and a minute later, he stomped upstairs. And Pascale followed. She knew how concerned he was about her.

They stayed in their room for a long time, talking, and came down to dinner late that night. Gwen had already said that she would cook for all of them, and she was ac-tually a better cook than Pascale. She even managed to talk Agathe into helping, and produced a very creditable cheese soufflé, and a gigot, a leg of lamb, which she cooked French style, while hopping over Agathe's herd of barking dogs. And when John and Pascale came down for dinner, he looked more relaxed than he had in days. He was surprisingly amorous with Pascale, who actually made him admit, after his fourth glass of wine, that he really did like France.

"Can I record this?" Robert teased him. "We'll have it typed up, and he can sign it as a statement. What about Pascale's mother? Do you like her too?"

"Of course not. I'm drunk, not crazy." They all laughed at him, and he sat back, smoking his cigar, and holding Pascale's hand. She seemed better than she had in days. And everyone relaxed and had a pleasant evening. Eric and Diana were on good terms, and Robert and Gwen looked very much in love. It was a good group of good people, and fast friends. And despite the new face in their midst, everyone seemed to have adjusted. After nearly two weeks with them, they had finally accepted Gwen. More than that, they had come to like her, and by the end of the evening, they were all talking about renting Coup de Foudre again the following year.

"I'm bringing plumbing fixtures and parts from New York next time," John said firmly. He had had a running battle with his toilet ever since they'd arrived. Pascale said it gave him something to do while he complained.

"It's been a great three weeks," they all agreed. Everyone

had finally relaxed, and they all seemed to be on the right track. Robert and Gwen with their budding romance, and Eric and Diana with their marital repairs, and John had managed to survive nearly choking on a piece of sausage. There had been no casualties, no losses, no one missing in action. It was a definite success.

And the last week sped by them all too quickly. They swam, they sailed, they talked, they slept. Pascale was still dragging her stomach bug around, but she seemed better, and John was less frantic about it. All they could think of in the last few days was how much they hated to go home.

They cooked lobsters on their last night, and two of them got loose and attacked Agathe's dogs. She ran screaming from the kitchen with all of them under her arms, and Gwen was left to fend for herself. She had volunteered to do the cooking, as usual, as long as the others helped her clean up. They had dinner in the garden that night, at the only decent table they'd salvaged when they got there, Diana set it with a tablecloth she'd bought to take home, and Pascale did the flowers. And when they sat down, Eric poured the champagne. The dinner Gwen had prepared was exquisite, and had been delicious. They were savoring every moment of it afterward, as the sun set slowly, and John lit a cigar, and Robert poured Château d'Yquem. John nearly fainted as he drank it, knowing what it had cost.

"It's a sin to drink anything this expensive," he said, loving every minute of it. It was like melted gold.

"I thought we'd split the price of the bottle three ways," Robert teased. He had bought it for all of them. He knew Gwen loved Château d'Yquem, and he didn't mind the expense, to spoil her. She had been such a good sport, and done the lion's share of the cooking, once Pascale got sick, and she had been a good friend to all of them.

"I really hate to go back," Diana admitted, and Gwen talked about the movie she was about to make in L.A. She was going to be there for four months. Probably till Christmas, but Robert had already said he'd come out on weekends, and she was going to try to get to New York as often as she could. She was going into rehearsal the following week, and they had already adjusted the rehearsal schedule for her, so she could spend the last week in St Tropez with him.

"I guess it'll be kind of nice to see the kids," Diana admitted. But she hadn't really missed them all month, she'd been too busy trying to put things back together with Eric, and to the others at least, it looked as though they had.

"I can hardly wait to see mine," Pascale said casually, and everyone looked blank, and wondered if she was drunk.

"You don't have any," Eric said with an amused expression. "But you can have ours anytime."

"I have my own, thank you very much," Pascale said, looking amused.

"I think her stomach bug has gone to her brain," Eric laughed as he poured her a little more Yquem.

And then she looked at John with a very Gallic smile. "We're having a baby," she said softly, "that's my 'stomach bug.' The doctor told me the day I went back with Gwen. But John and I wanted to wait and surprise you on the last night." The others looked at them, stunned, as Pascale beamed. "I will be forty-eight when it is born, and I don't care if I look like its grandmother. This is our little miracle. It finally happened. I've never been so happy in my life." The others knew how hard they had tried to have children, and what it meant to her, and it brought tears to Diana's eyes.

"Oh Pascale . . ." Diana rushed around the table to hug and kiss her, and Robert and Eric did the same, and then Gwen hugged her and told her how happy she was for her. She said it had crossed her mind once, but she didn't want to be rude and ask.

They toasted her with the Château d'Yquem and then brought out more champagne, but Pascale stuck with the Yquem, while John proudly handed out cigars to everyone, but this time Pascale didn't indulge. She knew that smoking a cigar just then would have pushed her over the edge.

"Well, not to steal Pascale's thunder," Diana said, glancing at Eric.

"You're pregnant too?" John looked stunned, and everyone laughed.

"No, we're staying married. I think Coup de Foudre did it for us." Love at First Sight. The perfect name for their run-down villa, and the things that had happened there that month. "That's pretty good news as far as we're concerned." Eric squeezed her hand, and the others cheered.

"That's the best news!" Robert said heartily, and Gwen looked pleased. Diana had already told her that she had had a hand in that.

"Which leaves us," Robert said. "Since everyone is making announcements . . . we have some news to share with you. . . . We're going to get married next spring, if Gwen hasn't gotten bored with me by then, or decided she can't stand the rest of you. You've been a hell of a lot of work for her, she had to save Eric and Diana's marriage, John's life . . . and me. I think she ought to get another Oscar for all the work she's done." He was teasing, but there was some truth in it as well. "Just so she doesn't have to deliver Pascale's baby. When is it due by the way?"

"March, I think. I'm still a little confused about that."

"I think we're going to get married in May or June, after Gwen finishes a picture she's doing next spring with

Danielle Steel

Tom Cruise and Brad Pitt. If she doesn't run off with one of them, she'll marry me."

"There's no danger of that," she said, smiling shyly, and looking around the table at her new friends. "You've all been so good to me . . . it was so wonderful to be here . . . and I love Robert so much . . . " she said, with tears in her eyes. It had been an emotional evening, an important month. It was a new beginning for all three couples, new lives for each of them, and something they had shared once again. Gwen felt like one of them now, and as Robert pulled her close to him and kissed her, the others smiled, watching them, as the sun set in a fiery golden ball over St Tropez.